Bi-Curious 2:

Life After Sadie

Bi-Curious 2:

Life After Sadie

Natalie Weber

www.urbanbooks.net

Urban Books, LLC
78 East Industry Court
Deer Park, NY 11729

Bi-Curious 2: Life After Sadie Copyright © 2012
Natalie Weber

ISBN 13: 978-1-60162-486-4
ISBN 10: 1-60162-486-7

First Printing March 2012
Printed in the United States of America

10 9 8 7 6 5 4 3 2 1

This is a work of fiction. Any references or similarities to actual events, real people, living, or dead, or to real locales are intended to give the novel a sense of reality. Any similarity in other names, characters, places, and incidents is entirely coincidental.

Distributed by Kensington Publishing Corp.
Submit Wholesale Orders to:
Kensington Publishing Corp.
C/O Penguin Group (USA) Inc.
Attention: Order Processing
405 Murray Hill Parkway
East Rutherford, NJ 07073-2316
Phone: 1-800-526-0275
Fax: 1-800-227-9604

Bi-Curious 2:

Life After Sadie

An erotic novel

by

Natalie Weber

Acknowledgments

First and foremost, I would like to thank God for granting all the opportunities sent my way. Because of You, I am truly blessed.

To all my fans, I just want to say that you are the best. Y'all showed me 'nough love as a new author. For that, I am humbled and forever in your debt. Thank you, everyone.

Thank you to my brother-in-law, Carl Weber, for the push and the confidence you have in me. It means a lot.

Thanks to Lonnie Baskerville, I have one of the hottest covers out. Your work is definitely appreciated.

I certainly can't forget my editors: Diane and Alanna. Just saying thank you seems so small. I can't tell how much I have learned just by your edits. Thank you, thank you!

A special thank you goes out to my husband. Thank you for taking over when I had deadlines to meet. Thanks for all those days you dealt with my nasty attitude because I stayed up all night and had no sleep. Thanks, baby. If I didn't have you, I don't know where I would be. I love you unconditionally.

Finally, to my boys: Thank you for not hating me when I ignored you completely. When you are older, you will understand fully. Words cannot express how much I love you.

Prologue

It was unusually warm on the streets of Detroit nightlife. Serenity just got out of a forever-lasting sex session. She was worn out and worked over. She couldn't remember the last time she felt that good. Serenity glanced at the time. She had time to get to Cass. Her clit was throbbing, and she needed to calm it. She knew exactly who to call.

"Hello," she spoke into the phone.

"Hey, didn't I just leave you? What, you miss me already?"

"Somethin' like that. . . . Umm, I want to get off. I'm still feelin' your touch," Serenity didn't hold back.

"Hold on. Let me pull over."

"Hurry, baby, 'cause I really need you. . . . I want your tongue to lick every inch on my body. You know I need it. You know I want it. Why do you like to do this to me? I'm all wet, and my nipples are hard as hell," Serenity said in a seductive tone.

"Ummm . . . You touching them? I know how you like to glide your fingers over them when they're hard. Is your pussy wet, baby? I want to taste you right now," the voice urged lustfully, wanting to touch Serenity's smoothly shaved pussy.

"Oh really? You know I'm horny. All I can think of"—she moved her fingertips in a circular motion over her protruding nipples—"is your sweet juice in my mouth." Serenity eased her legs open and inched her skirt up a little more.

"Hmm, I can't wait for you to put me into your mouth and suck me dry. I want to make you feel *good*. I want you to cum hard all over me."

"Yeah, baby, is that what you want me to do? You want to make me feel good? How good do you want me to feel? Mmmm-mmmm," Serenity cooed as she slowly rubbed her clit. She wanted to cum and didn't want to wait. She wanted a prelude before she headed out the door.

"Ahhh, you rubbing that clit, aren't you? I can't wait to caress your breasts and suck on those big nipples. . . . I'm gonna lick you from behind and wait for you to cum in my mouth . . ."

"Ohhhhh . . . You know I like that . . .mmmm . . . baby . . . You know what I like . . . am cumming . . . keep talking . . ." Serenity's fingers began to move faster and her climax was quickly approaching.

"Ahhh, you like it when I talk dirty to you, don't you? You want me to fuck you, don't you? You gonna cum for me, baby? I want to taste all your sweet cum in my mouth."

"Ohhhhh . . . Ohhhhh . . . Yeah, baby, that's what I'm talking about. I love it when you fuck me. I want you . . . Oh damn, baby . . . Oh shit . . . Here it comes, baby . . . ahhh-hhh . . ." Serenity let out a loud sigh, not even realizing how loud she was. She lay there just breathing into the phone, taking in all the goodness that just exploded between her legs.

A minute went by.

"Serenity, you still there?"

"Yeah, baby, I needed that." Serenity let out a slight laugh.

"Happy I was the one you called. What do you think of coming to my house later?"

"I want to, but how am I going to cover that up?" Serenity asked as the feeling of wanting more was simmering between her legs.

"The nice thing about it is that you don't have to. I think you can come up with somethin'. Besides, I don't think I could sleep without you tonight. Please make it work. You know you want it. And, you definitely know *I* want it. Listen, I'm heading back to work for a few; then I'll hit you up in a couple of hours to see what you gonna do. Serenity, please don't disappoint me. I'll talk to you later."

Serenity hung up the phone, praying that she hadn't made the second-biggest mistake in her life.

"She'll be there by ten," a male voice said.

"A'ight," the callous voice let out a laugh, then continued, "just make sure yo' ass proceed as usual. After a few weeks, come see me to get the rest of your money."

"One," said the male voice before hanging up the phone. He knew everything had to be perfect not to raise any suspicions.

"Ay-yo, Stuckey, did you see that bitch?" he questioned.

"Yeah, right on time," Stuckey replied.

"Yeah, too bad that bitch ain't gonna enjoy her stay!" He laughed and closed his phone shut, then took his time and drove to Serenity's location.

Arriving thirty minutes later, he parked on the opposite side of the hotel. He quickly opened his phone and pressed redial. "Yo, she still in there, right?"

"Yeah, I see you, my nigga. So the whip will be parked in the alley next to the hotel. The key is in the glove. I'ma go do what I got to do. Know what I mean?" Stuckey questioned eagerly, wanting to leave.

"Yeah, a'ight." His voice was low.

"Nigga, what, you changed your mind? Look I'ma go handle this shit, then I'ma take my black ass somewhere so you can't call me to do shit," Stuckey smoothly joked, not trying to stir up any more anger. He knew this was personal, and he was already knee-deep in it. He just wanted this shit over with.

"Just fucking with you, pussy! Take a trip; we'll talk, one!" He closed his phone and placed black leather gloves on his hands. Before stepping out of the car, he took a rag out of his pocket and wiped the car clean, eliminating all traces of his fingerprints. The car was stolen so he left the keys in the ignition. He already planned for someone to retrieve the car and get rid of it.

Dressed in all-black with not a sound in his footsteps, he crept into the building and cautiously walked up three flights of stairs before reaching the floor. Before he exited the staircase, he took a deep breath and a sinister smile spread across his face. Reaching into his jacket pocket, he took out the key card. When opening the exit door, he looked in both directions down the hall before stepping into the hallway. Quickly, he turned right and walked a few steps to a door marked FIVE, where he put his ear to the door and heard soft music playing. He slid the key card over the doorknob and slowly opened the door. As he entered, he smelled the air full of sweet sex. As he looked around, he saw clothes thrown all over the place. His hand groped his crotch. He felt himself getting turned on by smell of pussy in the air. *Maybe I'll get some too,* he thought.

Creeping slowly, he heard soft moans coming from another room. The closer he got, the more turned on he became. The moaning became louder. The door was not closed, and the room was dimly lit. He stood watching Serenity feeding her pussy into her lover's face with her face against the headboard. Her ass jiggled just right. His dick instantly became harder.

He inched closer without a sound and waited for that moment of ecstasy. As soon as he heard that moan of pure pleasure, his hand reached out and instantly snatched Serenity off the bed and threw her onto the floor toward a corner of the room against the wall.

"Ahhhhhh! What the fuck? Call the police! Call nine-one-one, quickly!" Serenity screamed, hoping that there was no one else with the intruder.

"Oh no, bitch, ain't nobody"—his hands gripped her throat—"calling not a motherfuckin' soul," he said in a calm, deadly voice. He reached above her head and turned up the light in the room.

Serenity tried to get up and run, but he used his huge hands to slap her down like a bothersome fly. She tried to study his face to figure out where, or if, she knew this person. *I don't see my baby*, she scanned the room.

"Please, just take what you want and leave. I won't call the police. Please just leave us alone." Serenity began sobbing and covered her face.

"Ahhh, shut the fuck up, bitch. You was just screaming"—he waved his hands in front of his face like a little girl—"a fucking minute ago to call the police. Stop fuckin' lyin'. Ho, I don't want nothing from your ass. I already got my own, you fuckin' typical dumb trick. I ain't fuckin' here to rob you. Look at me, you cunt. Don't put your head down. Open yo' fucking eyes, bitch, or you want me to do it?"

Serenity turned around not lifting her head, removed her hands covering her face, and opened her eyes. Her tears made everything look cloudy, and her head was spinning. She slowly moved her head up enough to see this monster before she died.

"Don't I look"—he stepped back and flashed his famous smile—"a little familiar?"

She closed her eyes and began crying and wishing this was just another nightmare and she would wake up soon. She felt a soft hand gently wiping her tears. She was now inches from his face and spoke with sincerity. "I don't know you. We have never met before. I think you have the wrong person," she cried louder. "Please, let me go . . . please!"

"Bitch, what the fuck you mean you don't know me?" He smacked her hard, causing blood to spew from her lips.

"I don't know who the fuck you are! I have never seen you before. Please just let me go. I will—" Serenity's loud pleas were cut short by another smack across her face.

"Listen, baby girl, you took something from me that I will never be able to replace," he spoke in a low, sultry tone, almost seductive, "and that shit you gonna fuckin' pay for."

"But . . . but . . . where is . . ." Serenity stuttered to plead with him.

"Your man? Let's just say you ain't with him anymore! What you think? I wasn't gonna come after you?" he chuckled. "You might as well come give me a taste of that pussy too! I want to see why my sister died for it!" he lashed out, hovering over her naked body, staring at her neatly shaved pussy.

Serenity couldn't believe that her life would end this way. *How could this happen, again?* she wondered.

Serenity had worked hard to forget the awful events in her recent past, but now they were being thrown at her. It seemed that Sadie was reaching out from the grave to try to kill her again, this time through her brother, Shawn P. Serenity thought Tootsie was the person she had to fear because she would never rest 'til she got even with Serenity for Sadie's death. Yes, Tootsie was locked up because Sadie tricked her into murdering Serenity's old boyfriend, Rock. But Serenity knew she'd be free sometime; that was why she and her sister, Carla, had come to a Detroit to start a new life. Instead, it turned out it was Shawn who had come to kill her, but how had he found her? Had this man she thought could bring her some happiness left her alone here fighting for her life? It was a nightmare, and she was terrified as she stared into the eyes of a man ready to make her life a distant memory.

Now, Serenity faced certain death from the man who stood before her.

Chapter 1

Six months earlier . . .

"Yeah, baby, bring it here. Let mama taste it."

"Keep talking like that, bitch, that's right . . . Daddy got it right here. . . . Open fucking wide . . ." the sweaty, oversized drunk said, spewing his juice into her mouth. He made sure every last drop was swallowed, then pushed her to the side as if he was disgusted. He quickly pulled up his pants and reached into his pocket. His hand appeared gripping a wad of cash, slowly peeling off a few bills, then throwing them at her.

She heard the door slam, then stood to her feet and glanced at the mirror. *Is this what you have become? Are you this low?*

Tootsie wanted to end it all. She didn't think about where her life was going. She stared into the mirror trying to figure out how she got on this train heading for the town of Shits-Ville. She looked past her image and saw herself several months earlier in jail. It was as though she were living that time all over again.

What the fuck is happening to me? I can't do time because of that bitch Serenity. She made me kill Rock. If that bitch would of just stayed with her man and stayed the fuck away from my love, this shit wouldn't be happening. I gotta get that bitch. She has to understand she can't get away with killing my Sadie without consequences.

"Do you think you can help me? I can't go to jail! I've been sitting in here for the past year waiting for this trial to start. Listen, I know who you want, and I can help you get her. Just get me the fuck out of this bitch and I will clue you in."

She sat there not knowing what would happen next. She sat near a window overlooking the facility's garden area surrounded with brightly colored tulips and orderlies walking in and out of the facility. How could she have known that she was about to join the most elite of the streets in the worst way ever desired. Stupid bitch ran through her mind a thousand times wondering if she could really pull this shit off.

"A'ight I'ma roll with you, shorty. But don't think this shit will be easy or as quick as you think. So you got to take it real slow in here and don't talk to nobody but the muthafucker I send from this point on." Shawn P slowly rose from his seat, brushed his hands down the front of his pants, and walked away.

She can't believe these stupid-ass muthafuckers. They really thought she was crazy. She had the best lawyer in town thanks to her mass manipulation and knowing a muthafucker's weakness—revenge. When she was arrested, the court-appointed attorney was worthless. Now that the most respected defense attorney within a hundred-mile radius had taken her case, days to come seemed to look a little brighter. Mr. Robert Hilton gave her the fuel she needed to get through the trial. He painted a serene picture of a young, misguided woman who went into college a scholar and got sucked into a fast life with emotional dilemmas.

She sat in that crazy house praying that that fucking death penalty or life shit wouldn't happen. She hoped to be facing time served, with some probation, of course. The fucking lawyer had better do his fuck-

ing thing 'cause she would hate to wild the fuck out and get herself shot by one of those court officers—She was not going back to that box.

Maybe she shouldn't get involved with that nigga, Shawn P, but she knew exactly what and who he wanted. She could be the only one that could get him close enough to her. She knew what Serenity's weakness really was.

Today was the day, and she was scared shitless. Today she would see the judge at a hearing closed to the public and get her life served on a silver platter or juiced with toxins. Her heart pumped with pure adrenaline. It felt like she snorted lines of that Columbian good stuff. The court officers seated her next to Mr. Hilton at the defendant's table in the courtroom. The pumping of her heart was so loud in her head she didn't even notice when the judge walked in. Mr. Hilton tapped on her shoulder. Everything went silent, and she couldn't feel her legs. Her short life was passing before her. "Dear God, please have mercy on my soul," she whispered a desperate prayer.

The gavel sounded and a strong, loud voice began. "Mr. Hilton, I understand that you have reached a plea."

"What the fuck you mean—" I turned quickly and screamed, almost flipping the defense table.

"Mr. Hilton, do you need a moment with your client?" Judge Marley Staples asked, quite irritated at the outburst.

"Yes, please, Your Honor, five minutes will do."

The judge recessed for fifteen minutes.

"Excuse me, but this whole fucking time you been playing my ass. Are you fucking stupid?" I growled in a low tone.

"Tootsie, this is the best we can do. You will get some time served and won't get more than six years on parole. You will have to do an outpatient program at a psychiatric facility. Look, if we would've continued with this trial, your life would be in the hands of some people I really don't think you call your peers. You can take it or leave it. I walk out of here either way. What do you want to do?" Mr. Hilton sat back in the chair.

"So you mean, all this time you have been plotting behind my back. Trying to make sure my coffin was sealed tight, huh?" Tootsie looked around the half-empty courtroom and saw Shawn P in the very back.

"No, trust me, the quicker I get you out of this trial, the quicker I can move on and forget I ever came to visit you." Mr. Hilton looked around to watch the crowd and reporters shuffling back in.

"Fine, but I swear to fuckin' God my ass better be gettin' the fuck outta this bitch soon," she gritted through her teeth. As mad as she was, the most she could do was hope for the best outcome.

Judge Marley Staples banged the gavel once more. *"Okay, are we all on the same page, Mr. Hilton?"*

"Yes, please excuse the earlier outburst. We are ready to proceed," Mr. Hilton apologized.

"Very well, then. Okay, it looks like we have a plea accepted by both parties . . . ummm . . . uh-huh . . . Okay, Ms. Richards, please stand. Do you accept and understand this plea?"

"Yes, I do, Your Honor," Tootsie replied and looked back at Shawn P.

"You understand you will be attending a sixteen-month outpatient psychiatric facility and paroled for ten years following your release?" Judge Staples questioned.

"Ten years?" she jumped back in shock. Tootsie shot a look at Mr. Hilton, making him inch back immediately, fearing she would come after him. She took a deep breath and said, *"Yes, Your Honor, I understand ten years."* Her voice hinted at her disappointment.

"You also understand that you will be subjected to random drug testing and home searches for such drugs? And, the aftereffects of a positive result of such testing or searches?"

"Yes, Your Honor, I do," Tootsie stated.

"And, finally, you know you are not allowed to leave the district of Washington, D.C., until you finish your outpatient program and get final approval from the parole board?" Judge Staples took her glasses off, put her papers down, then reached for her gavel.

"Yes, Your Honor," Tootsie replied with a great big smile on her face. Her mind was clear now. Shawn P came through for her. The weight on her chest was lifted, but she knew her indebtedness would come with a price.

"Okay, so be it." Judge Staples banged the gavel and retreated to her chambers while the courtroom dispersed.

Before the court officer removed Tootsie, she shook Mr. Hilton's hand very tightly. *"So how long do you think it will be before I will be able to get me out of here and assigned to an outpatient center?"* Tootsie asked with happiness in her voice.

"It's going to take a few hours; then you will be able to be on your way. Please don't forget you will only have twenty-four hours to see your parole officer. You will receive your release papers with all that information." Then Mr. Hilton packed all his papers into his briefcase as the officer reached for Tootsie's arm to usher her out of the courtroom.

***

Tootsie snapped out of her trance and walked over to the other side of the bed. She saw the money scattered all over the floor. Staring at the money, her hands didn't want to extend to retrieve it any faster. She wanted to drop to her knees and cry until her tears dried up. She didn't see her life like this—it was supposed to be with Sadie.

The only person that I want dead now more than ever is that bitch—Serenity, Tootsie thought walking to the bathroom.

"Yo, what up? Can you tell me when we doin' this? I want to do this now. I can't wait any longer. You got me turning tricks and all type of shit that wasn't supposed to go down. What the fuck, Shawn?" Tootsie wiped her eyes and lit a cigarette, nearly singeing her eyelashes.

"Shorty, when you walked out with no cuffs, you owed me big time, so just fall the fuck back and enjoy the only life you will have until I say, 'no more.'" Shawn P spoke effortlessly and hung up the phone without any calming consolation prize.

This muthafucker gotta come correct. Now it's time to reassess the situation, 'cause I can't be having this muthafucker thinking he can just do anything or keep doing this shit to me, Tootsie thought as she blew smoke up into the air.

Chapter 2

"Okay, I know you didn't wanna leave Chicago, but we needed a new start. No fuckin' detectives, court, or reporters out front knowin' our every fuckin' move. That shit wasn't good for business, if you know what I mean. Don't worry. Like I told you, we still got Momma house. We just have tenants now. So, I rented this house out here in Detroit," Carla said as she burst through the door, dropping their luggage upon entering.

"Damn, when you told me that we were going to Detroit, I wasn't too thrilled, but you're right. We do need to start somewhere fresh and forget the past year. That reminds me, I tried calling the lawyer to find out how many years that bitch got, but he ain't callin' me back. Well, I guess it really doesn't matter anymore," Serenity said, scoping the house out with her eyes.

"Oh yeah, well, I called him the other day. He said she got twenty to life in a maximum facility. Besides, the case is finished," Carla told a bold-faced lie. "Okay, sis, since all that Sadie stuff is behind us, can you tell me something?" Carla asked shyly. She didn't want Serenity to shut her down. "So, tell me which team are you really batting for?" Carla took a seat on the sofa.

"Huh? What?" Serenity was caught off guard with her sister's question.

"Don't 'what' me, Serenity. You know exactly *what* I'm asking. Are you into chicks now or not?" Carla asked again.

"Well, since you want to be all in my business, no, I'm not into chicks. My experience with that is over. I want dick and dick only. Those chicks got way too much drama for me." Serenity took a seat next to Carla on the sofa. "Disappointed?"

"Honestly, yes. Not 'cause you only want dick now, but 'cause you didn't feel like you could tell me that you felt that way about women. I blame myself for all this happening to you. I should'a known and warned you about what really goes on over at that school." Carla looked over at Serenity and grabbed her hand. "Listen, I want you to know I am here for you no matter who you fucking or sucking. If you think you got a problem, please, please, come to me, sis, please. Okay?"

"Since when you all mushy and shit? I know I should'a told you about those feelings, but you don't have to worry about that anymore. If I got a problem, I promise you, sis, I will holla at you without hesitation. Now, I'm fuckin' starvin'. Let's go get something to eat," Serenity reassured her sister.

"A'ight. I guess this luggage and shit can get done when we return. Do you mind coming with me to check out this spot I have been hearin' about? It's a restaurant, and after eleven, it turns into a lounge or somethin' like that. The food is supposed to be good. What you say?" Carla asked.

"I don't care, but they food better be good." Serenity stood up and rushed to the door.

Carla followed behind Serenity, and they both hopped into the car on their way to the restaurant. When they reached the restaurant, they both recited the name out loud. "All Things Good."

Serenity looked at Carla and said, "It better be."

"Come on, we won't know 'til we get in there," Carla nudged Serenity.

When they entered, they looked at the crowd and smiled at each other. "Well, it gots to be good, sis. Look at the crowd," Carla said.

"Okay, but now how long do you think we'll have to wait? Damn, I knew we should'a just went to the chicken spot." Serenity sucked her teeth. "I'm out front 'cause this is going to take forever."

"Serenity, come on. Just hang for a minute and let me find out how long. Damn, sometimes you are so fuckin' spoiled," Carla shot back.

Serenity glared at Carla and headed for the front door. She hated when her sister was right. When she reached the entrance, a gentleman almost bumped into her. His smile caused her to forget her sister's comment.

"Oh, pardon me, Miss, I didn't see you," a six foot three man with caramel-toned skin and a muscular frame spoke. His eyes met Serenity's and an instant attraction arose. He gazed at her unblemished face and eyes that would make any man's heart throb.

Serenity stood still and momentarily lost her voice. His presence was inviting and drop-dead gorgeous. His hazel eyes and caramel-colored skin stopped her in her tracks.

"A'ight, Serenity, let's go to the chicken spot. It's an hour-long wait, so I guess we'll try another time," Carla said, looking at the man standing in their way. "Come on, what's the deal? Can you move outta the way, man?"

"I can get you a table right now. Please, don't leave." He smiled at them.

"Yeah, whatever, man. Let's go." Carla's voice became loud.

"Oh, I'm sorry. Are you two together?" He looked at Carla and noticed her possessiveness.

"No, not at all." Serenity rolled her eyes.

"Okay, well, at least let me introduce myself. My name is Cassidy Peters, but everyone calls me Cass. I'm one of the owners and would love for you both to have dinner here, on me. Do you like jazz? The band will be here in half an hour or so. What do you say?" Cassidy stared at Serenity, hoping she would say yes.

"We good. Come on, let's go," Carla quickly answered.

"Cass, I would love to find out if the food really is good. Carla, are you staying or going to the chicken spot?" Serenity asked her sister with a smile.

"Ain't that some shit . . . whatever. Okay, Cass, where we sitting?" Carla questioned.

"Follow me. I will show you to the best seats in the house. By the way, can I get your names?" Cass smiled.

"It's Serenity, and this is my sister Carla," Serenity smiled.

Cass walked through the crowd throwing "hellos" and handshakes to what seemed like every person they passed along the way. He finally seated them at a corner table with a card marked RESERVED on top. He removed the card and motioned a waitress over.

"Please, take care of my new friends, and everything is on the house. Don't worry, I'll take care of you later," Cass told the waitress. "Now, ladies, enjoy your dinner and have a great night." Cass left the table without saying another word.

Serenity didn't know what to think. Her mind was fluttering with questions. *Who is this dude? And, why is he being so nice to me?* She didn't know who he was. She wasn't in Chicago anymore.

Cass had plenty of paper. His first taste of paper came from the streets of Brooklyn. Supplying bricks to all of the hustlers in the borough gained notoriety in the hood.

He got smart, stacked his paper, and quickly opened a string of nightclubs throughout the city. When the police started infiltrating his empire, he escaped with the help of his sister. They invaded Detroit and slowly started building relationships with the moneymakers of the city. He purchased a mansionlike catering hall and renovated it into a restaurant with a nightclub to keep his paper up. He became a star among the night scene in Detroit. He entertained many women and discovered it was easy to manipulate most.

He thought about that as he moved away from the table. Women were all after the same thing . . . status and money. They were looking to be upgraded. Serenity had no idea that he was well-known to many, and he wanted to keep it that way.

"Okay, so I see you got your game back," Carla snickered as she took the menu from the waitress.

"Ladies, take a look at the menu and decide. I'll be right back to take your order. Can I get you any drinks?" the waitress asked.

"Actually, you can bring us a bottle of Patrón Silver and some limes. Thanks," Carla said.

"Can you bring a glass of lemonade as well," Serenity added.

After the waitress left the table Serenity said, "Damn, Carla, I know this shit is free, but you didn't have to order that. Damn, you greedy," Serenity laughed.

"Listen, you got to let niggas know you ain't a cheap date and you used to the fine things in life. Trust me," Carla replied as she scanned the room for anyone she knew.

"Whatever, Carla. But, damn, he sure is fine. I hope he comes back." Serenity stared at Cass mingling about the room. "Look, the band is setting up, and might I say this table looks like it's the best seat in this place."

"All right, don't wet your panties just yet. Let me do some research on this Cassidy before you venture off into his world," Carla said.

"Yeah, okay. But we definitely have to come back here, even if the food ain't good." Serenity noticed the waitress returning with their bottle. "Thank you."

"Have you ladies decided?" the waitress asked, ready to take their order.

"Actually, can you bring us your best of everything. Thanks." Carla smiled at the waitress noticing her tight white shirt exposing her hard nipples.

The waitress smiled back at Carla giving her a hint that her interest was wanted. The waitress wrote her number down on her order pad and gave it to Carla. "I'll be back with the best in the house."

"I see someone else got some game too," Serenity laughed.

Their waitress arrived with their food shortly after Serenity and Carla had consumed several shots of Patrón. They both looked at the amount of food placed in front of them. There were several plates of every-thing—collard greens, baked mac and cheese, barbecue chicken, ribs, yams, brisket, fried chicken and shrimp, catfish, and corn bread made in a skillet like their mother used to make. Neither knew where to start.

Cassidy stole a few glances at Serenity while she enjoyed the food but decided on not going over to the table to make any conversation. He wanted her in every way possible but didn't want to blow it by asking her for her number. He thought, *If she's interested, she'll come back. I ain't chasin' nothing!*

Chapter 3

After being in their new home a week and enrolling Serenity in the community college nearby, Carla looked at her stash and quickly started to formulate a plan to re-up. She knew she couldn't call Shawn P, but maybe that Iris chick from Rock's funeral could help. When Iris made her appearance at the funeral, she was discreet, but she also made it clear that she could help her. Carla didn't understand back then, but now it was clear. Through her informants in the streets of Chicago, she figured out that Iris was the other chick Rock was mainly fucking, and she also was the mastermind behind the entire weed service he had going. From what info she did gather, Iris was the chick with the hookups for everything bad.

Through Carla's connections with all the big Chicago players, she found out just how bad Iris really was. Her hustle was on point and always growing. She made drug deals with the biggest, and her money was definitely deeper than any normal hustler. Iris played the game well. Her connections with the Columbian Mafia and the Polish mob brought her great respect all around. Iris was known to use her strong ties to earn trust with local dealers and use them to advantage with her bigger affiliates.

When the trial started, the publicity made Carla's hustle harder than ever. Her normality became restricted by the constant eyes on Serenity. After weeks of hospital visits, then sitting in the courtroom for what seemed like months, not to hear a jury say "guilty" was heart wrenching. She couldn't let her sister know that Tootsie was taking a plea instead of going to jail for the rest of her life. While the jury was deliberating, the lawyer came to her stating that Tootsie was going to cop a plea instead of getting what she deserved. Carla decided it was best for Serenity not to know and informed the lawyer that Serenity was leaving the state for good. Carla hated herself for not protecting Serenity before. She thought back on all that she would of, should of, could of—but didn't—do.

I'm her protector. How could I've been so blind? There were signs that shit was wrong. I should'a just went with my gut and told her she couldn't go to that school in the first fuckin' place. Why didn't I? Carla looked at her mother's picture on her dresser with tears in her eyes.

"Mama, please don't be mad at me. She didn't let me in. She didn't tell me anything. I'm so sorry, Mama." Her cheeks were wet. She pulled the bottom of her shirt up to wipe her face. Carla's guilt was heavy and weighed like fifty strong-ass men standing on her shoulders. The thought of Serenity finding out that Tootsie wasn't in jail and was free to roam wherever she pleased kept her in a constant battle. She wanted to accumulate enough money so she could take Serenity away and tell her the truth, but like a parent, her role was clear: she had made sure Serenity was safe, and the less she knew, the better.

Carla searched the top of her dresser for the funeral pamphlet. She found it and hoped the number was still connected. *Well, let's see what she can do for me,* Carla thought as she dialed the number.

"Hello?" Iris answered, a bit confused.

"Hey, I'm Carla, Serenity's sister and—"

"No need to explain. I know who you are. When can we meet?" Iris cut her off.

"Well, I'm not sure . . . Chi-town ain't my home no more. You think you can come out to Detroit?" Carla asked.

"I'm actually in D.C., but I can be in Detroit by the weekend. We can meet then. I'll call you when I land." Iris hung up the phone, not wanting Carla to bombard her with questions.

Carla looked at the phone and said out loud, "What the fuck? She just hung up on me! She better be able to come correct when I see her."

After Iris hung the phone up, she quickly opened her laptop to book a flight to Detroit. She thought of what Sadie took from her—the only man she loved. She knew Sadie didn't pull the trigger, but she might as well have. Her slick and cunning ways tricked Tootsie into killing Rock, and now someone had to pay. *Serenity should pay for her mistake of ever involving herself with that bitch Sadie. She's the reason he got killed,* Iris thought.

Iris cared deeply for Rock, and she knew his entire relationship with Serenity was just a cover-up to make his intended football career well perceived. He loved to watch women with women and join in. After a year of helping Rock with moving weight in and out of the state lines, Iris developed feelings for him, although her only interest at the time had been women. But, she and Rock spent a lot of time together and really got to know each other from the inside and out.

After some time of traveling together and making some major money, Iris thought she would let him in on her little secret. One night, when they traveled to Maryland to connect with a grower for high-grade weed, Iris made a bet with him. She wanted to show him how curious and free women could be, even if they were straight. They went to a bar in Baltimore, and Iris engaged in many conversations with the opposite sex, but finally, she picked a group of women to talk to. First, she offered drinks to everyone, then conversed for a while. She quickly found out one of the women was bisexual, and the reminder of them were all straight. At the end of the night, she invited everyone back to the hotel room and offered more drinks and conversation. After the drinks flowed and the conversation got freaky, Rock was seduced into his first sexual experience with more than one woman.

Rock was shocked to know that he was the first guy to feel Iris's tight flesh. From that day forth, he and Iris were more than just business partners. Their bond was tighter than what they led everyone around them to believe. Rock always had a girlfriend, and so did Iris, but when the two would get together, they were in their own world. He always answered her calls no matter what, and she did the same. They were real with each other.

But, Serenity was ultimately to blame for having taken him from her, so Iris put together a plan to get even with her. Iris vowed Serenity would pay for her life-changing decisions. She had figured once everything went down with Sadie, that Carla would need a new supplier. Carla wasn't a big-time hustler, but her potential was there, and all Iris would have to do would be to push her into the right hands. Iris quickly picked up her phone and dialed a number. "Hey, you, how you been?"

"What up, mama? I'm always good when you call," a low, deep male voice said.

"Well, that's a good thing. Listen, I'ma be in your neck of the woods soon. Can we get together? I think I have something lined up for you," Iris said in her sweetest voice.

"All good, baby. You have only brought me good fortune, so when you wanna meet?" the man asked.

"I'ma take a late flight on Thursday night. You think you can pick me up from the airport?" Iris asked.

"Not a thing, anything for my girl. Just hit me with the info and I'll see you. Have you decided on your hotel?"

"Why? No, let me guess. I bet I could stay with you, right?" Iris laughed.

"Mama, you know it! But by your laughter I see you stick to your own kind. Look, you can't knock a nigga for tryin'." He laughed loudly.

"A'ight. I'ma send you the info. Talk to you soon." Iris pressed the END button on her phone and smiled.

"Six, eight, ten . . . fuck! That just ain't gonna work. Fuck!" Carla screamed out loud, counting the stacks of money. *Oh, just ain't gonna make it. This bitch Iris better be straight up. I got half a brick left. I definitely ain't trying to hustle that shit in these streets. If this chick is what I heard, then maybe, just maybe I could spin a little web and get her hooked like a fish,* Carla thought as she placed the money and the coke in the safe in her closet.

Carla knew she had to do something to get a strong connect. Her only real connect was Shawn P and now, since all that had happened between Serenity and his sister, Sadie, Carla's connects were weak. They came through sometimes, and other times just left a bitch standing there with bullshit talk when all they really wanted was her assets. She always came across that one nigga who thought he could make her go straight.

A few years back, she was introduced to Shawn P one night at a private party held in Detroit for some major playas. Shawn P was impressed with Carla's swag with the ladies. He saw that Carla had game; a strong one. She moved through the room with confidence talking to only a select few females; then she would leave the party. As Shawn P watched, those who she talked to would leave with her. His interest piqued when one of those elite women was a gorgeous Latina he wanted to leave with. Carla, at that time, didn't know how deep Shawn P was into his hustling. She later found out his connection with getting weight was a sure thing. After a few conversations and a few females she brought along for a good time, it became a secured connect. She would just make a trip to D.C. three times a month with a hottie or two, and her paper would build and multiply. It became comfortable, and then everything went up with a big bang.

This gotta work. It better fuckin' work. The words repeated in Carla's mind as she lay back on her bed and stared at the ceiling.

American 3998 @O'Hare International in 1 hr, Iris typed into her phone waiting to board her flight. A minute later a reply scrolled across her notification screen.

See you then

Her thoughts lay heavily on the outcome of her meeting. *Hope this nigga can handle my request and come through. If I could get Carla hooked in, I could probably get a little closer to Serenity. It's all about making money, and my cut comes straight off the top every time.* Suddenly a female voice interrupted her thoughts.

"Good afternoon, ladies and gentlemen. Thank you for flying with American Airlines today. At this time I would like to welcome all business and first-class members to board."

"Hey, good looking. Can I give you a ride?" His light hazel eyes stared at her with a smile.

"You know you can," Iris answered. "It's been a minute since I saw you last."

"Yeah, I know. Are you staying at the Ritz nearby?" He grabbed a Louis Vuitton Alizé travel bag and headed out of the airport to the parking lot. "Are you hungry? We can stop by my place and grab something if you like."

"Cass, now you know I can't stand that country food. Don't take no offense, but that's a heart attack on speed dial," Iris laughed.

He opened the passenger-side door to his stark white Porsche Panamera, then placed her luggage into the trunk and got into the driver's seat. "Come on, Iris, it ain't that bad. The joint is packed ever since you hooked me up with some fresh faces and the lounge idea."

"I told you if you continued with only food your crowd would be limited. Now, I bet you meet the most elite, young and old. I told you good things always come to those who wait," Iris said.

"So, do you just want to check into the hotel and we can have something to eat there?" Cass asked.

"Yeah, that would be cool." Iris leaned back and stared out of the window.

Cass glanced over at her. "What you doing on this side anyway? Is there a problem with the percentage?" His voice spoke with concern.

"Nah, I'm good with what I get for now. I actually have another . . . another offer for you," Iris replied.

"Well, you know I always like your offers. I always end up with fat pockets," he said smiling.

"Look, let's get it straight. This ain't nothing for your lounges or your brothel," Iris's voice was firm.

"What you talking about?" Cass asked uneasy. He couldn't help but think about the house he just recently purchased.

"Don't act dumb, Cass. You know I can't stand stupid, so cut the shit. I know about the whole setup in Gary with some of them girls I sent your way. I'm not here to negotiate my cut on that just yet"—she pointed her finger at him and smirked—"I'm here on some other shit. I believe you can help me out."

They pulled into the hotel's valet parking area. Cass stepped out of the car and told the valet attendant the bag was in the trunk. "You know I don't really get down like that anymore. It caused me too many problems. Nowadays, I like to keep it easy—food, liquor, and women."

"I see. Well, let me check in, and I'll be back down in fifteen. Then I can change your mind," Iris said with confidence.

Cass chuckled. "Damn, you sure is cocky, ain't ya?" He headed to the bar to wait for her return. His iPhone began to vibrate. "Hey, you, what up?"

"Yo, I can't come in tonight. I done won some NFL tickets for the preseason game against New England," a female voice said.

"Ahh, come on. I told you I had some shit to do tonight. How the fuck did you win tickets?" Cass looked at his watch, then took a drink.

"Why does that matter? Listen, I got 'em, and I'm going! Come on, whoever you with could probably use a drink and a little dancing hanging with your lame ass," she said with a sassy attitude.

"Who you going with?" Cass asked curiously.

"I'm going with one of my girls," she answered.

"Damn, when the fuck you gonna start talking about a dude? You always with them girls of yours involving yourself with they shit! You need some fucking dick in your life—"

"Whoa, brother, why you raising your voice? Listen, this is not the time. I got somewhere to go, and you already where you at. But you need to be at the restaurant by six 'cause the band wants their money up front. So, before my tongue gets to talking all types of cuss words, I'm saying good-bye." Heaven hung up quickly.

Damn, this meeting gonna have to be short and sweet, he thought as he took a seat by the bar. *Ever since she came back from college, my restaurant has truly been running smoothly thanks to her. My money from these streets hasn't been washed any cleaner. I guess that business degree was the best investment I made. But I can't help think why she can't get no man. I only see her with them same bitches from the hood. Why? I keep telling her to stop fucking with them. They ain't nothing but drama.* Cass's thoughts bounced around his head waiting for Iris's return.

Chapter 4

The day Heaven Peters graduated from college was the happiest day of her life. She was so tired of being away from her brother and her friends. After her mother died, she solely depended on her brother. Heaven never knew her father, and Cass was the closest person to a father figure she had. Her childhood was tough living in Detroit; she dodged bullets as she walked to school, ate cheap-ass takeout, and moved from house to house because the police were looking for her brother or someone her brother was dealing with. But, no matter where she was, Cass made sure her education was a priority.

It was her senior year in high school when Cass told her she had four more years to go. She thought after high school she would just be part of her brother's business, the restaurant. Heaven was surprised that her brother made her go to college. She didn't want to. She was comfortable with what she had. Her brother always provided her with anything she wanted; clothes, shoes, sneakers, phones, and whatever else was a trend. It was a bittersweet moment when he told her that she also was moving to go to school.

Ever since their mom died, she was never allowed to hang unsupervised with anybody who was male. Her brother didn't want her to be a victim to the drama. Heaven was grateful for her brother's overprotectiveness since most of her friends were dropouts and teenage moms. However, her interest in sex had increased since Cass set her free when she finally went to college.

Heaven soon found out that plenty of chicks experimented sexually while in college. But her interest wasn't always with males; it was women that got her juices flowing. All of that time around other beautiful black women could make you feel things you had never felt before. All different shapes of black women, sizes, scents, accents, hair colors, bald pussies, hairy ones . . . It was all a daily temptation.

Heaven remembered the first time she had seen her college roommate Neisha naked. Her breasts were so perky, and her dark nipples much bigger than her own. Water had dripped from her body as she stepped out of the shower. Neisha caught Heaven looking and didn't seem shy or bothered by it at all. Neisha even approached her that day and pinned her up against the bathroom door. Heaven was too reserved and shy to admit that she had felt moisture between her legs. Instead she mumbled, "I don't get down like that."

Neisha even put her hands underneath Heaven's nightgown and rubbed her wet pussy.

"But it looks like you want me too," she said.

Heaven was so nervous she thought that the entire dorm could hear her beating heart.

Neisha lifted her nightgown just above her waist, then pressed her naked body against Heaven's. "All you got to do is rock, Heaven . . . It's easy, and it feels so good," she said seductively. She began to rock her hips gently.

She was turning Heaven on because Heaven's eyelids were closing. Her hips started grinding lightly before she knew it. Her clit was awakening, and her juices starting flowing.

"See, it feels good, don't it?" Neisha whispered. "Nobody has to know. We can do this all the time, roomie," she said. Neisha never stopped moving her wet box in rhythm as her soft voice went over Heaven's ear.

Heaven swallowed a lump in her throat. "No, I mean . . . stop. I told you I don't get down like that," Heaven repeated, uncomfortable.

Neisha shrugged and smiled devilishly. "Well, let me know if you ever want to finish. I love virgin pussy."

"I'm not a virgin," Heaven protested, embarrassed.

"You've never been with anyone. . . . Your pussy gets too wet at the thought of sex. So I know virgin pussy when I feel it," Neisha schooled her.

That night, Heaven had her first sexual experience with a woman. The next day, she went to student housing and got switched to another dorm. All through college she avoided Neisha, but she always wanted more.

Her fear had held her back; she didn't want anyone to know, even if it was okay. At the same time, Heaven didn't know if she wanted a man, because she had never experienced one. She had one close call in high school, but it didn't get far because her brother was always around, and she didn't like the aggressiveness of the man. Finally, when she got into college, she got a taste of what she really liked—someone with soft skin and gentle hands.

Heaven was curious, yes, but to allow her brother to know about her wanting to be with women would not go down smoothly. College was supposed to be fun she remembered her brother telling her. He said this was the time to see who you really were as a person. *But would he disown me if being with women is what I really want?* she thought.

Heaven sat on her sofa contemplating how long she could keep her true feelings a secret. She shook her head trying to erase her growing problem. Heaven held the envelope with the tickets in her hand. *When did I enter this contest? Well, I hope the shit is legit. I guess the only way to find out is to go.* She stood up and grabbed her purse by the door and left.

Tootsie took her seat at Ford Field, section 106, row nine. Shawn P and Stuckey took their seats beside her. She was happy to be out of D.C. and hoped that turning tricks wasn't Shawn P's objective in getting her out to Detroit, risking her freedom. Tootsie wanted nothing more than to run like the wind, but she knew he would find her no matter where she went. She figured that he just paid off the parole officer. Her presumptions on why she was turning tricks back in D.C. became clearer. She sat back staring at the field. *He didn't want to lose any more paper. He done lost so much already with the trial he had to make some money back.* Her thoughts flowed. *Now that we're here, it must be time to get down to business. That explains the new look I got the first day of my arrival. But he hasn't said nothin' 'bout it. Why?*

"Yo, Stuckey, wave the chick over here," Shawn P said looking around, scanning the crowd.

He wanted to make sure his special guest was in attendance. He found out through sources that Cass was seeing Serenity, and he was hoping she was a football fan. Maybe he would be able to use Cass's sister to convince him that he had no choice but to help get Shawn what he wants.

"Yeah, yeah, I got you. I want a drink myself," Stuckey added. The woman came over with a smile to take their drink order.

Tootsie placed her order and looked at Stuckey. She saw him in a different light. He was laughing, talking, and joking. He wasn't usually like this around her. He hardly talked to her unless it was to ask her what she wanted to eat or drink. Since Shawn P told Tootsie she was leaving D.C., Stuckey had been with her every step of the way.

Stuckey was not the type of person to mix pleasure with business, but after spending a week with Tootsie, his manhood was coming into question. Tootsie's petite body was fine in every way. Her short auburn, blond-highlighted hair rested slightly below her earlobes. Her brown caramel skin was unblemished. Tootsie's perky breasts and phat ass would drive any man crazy.

He knew that she liked women mainly, but on occasions she would fuck with a nigga. He didn't care that she was trickin'. In his mind, she was just making her money the only way she could. After keeping an eye on her for the past week, Stuckey wanted to get at her in the worst way. He didn't want Shawn P to know that his feelings were beginning to build so he always kept it cold as ice with her when Shawn P wasn't around. He didn't need her to blow anybody's spot up because she wanted out of whatever deal she had with Shawn P.

Tootsie looked around the crowd. Her eyes landed on a beautiful heart-shaped ass. Her long black hair showed her team spirit with a bright blue streak down the middle. Tootsie's eyes were glued. She couldn't see her face until the woman stood up and walked out of the aisle toward the bathroom. Tootsie's mouth watered looking at her smooth light skin as she walked by her.

Shawn P watched the entire scene unfold when Tootsie peeped Heaven. He definitely didn't intend for Tootsie to be smitten with her, but this might just work in his benefit.

Tootsie looked at Shawn P. He sent her a look which surprised her. She understood but didn't know why. To Tootsie, she was a random chick attending a football game. Her tight jeans and cutoff Lion's football jersey made the men behind her whistle like she was prime rib. She smiled.

"Um, Stuckey, you better go with her. Son, don't let her out your sight," Shawn P spoke.

"Yeah, a'ight." Stuckey stood up and looked at Tootsie, "Come on. Let's make this quick. I don't want to miss the kickoff," he said with some annoyance in his voice.

Tootsie walked out of the row and headed to the bathroom with Stuckey on her heels. *Damn, I just can't get away from this nigga. Fuck, he got to be gay or something. I can't believe he ain't make a move for me yet, even with the stunt I pulled last night. Shit, I practically walked outta my room naked, and he didn't even flinch,* Tootsie thought.

As they entered the corridor that led to the restrooms, she turned around abruptly and Stuckey nearly fell on top of her. She grabbed him quickly and placed her lips on his. He jumped back and looked around.

"There is no one around, so why don't you join me in the bathroom?" Tootsie said in her soft, sexiest voice.

"Nah, nah, I ain't . . ." Stuckey couldn't make his words come out fast enough.

"Straight? I *knew* you were gay. Shit, any straight nigga would want to tap this free of charge!" Tootsie put one hand on her hip and the other on her collarbone displaying her assets.

Stuckey got closer to her face and grabbed both of her hands, then held them behind her back while he parted her lips with his tongue. Tootsie struggled to loosen his grip, but that only lasted five seconds. He let go of her hands and continued to play with her tongue.

His hands slowly rubbed against her nipples, allowing them to harden. She nudged his dick and felt its strong stance. Before she could start stroking his cock like she wanted, she heard someone yell out, "Get a fucking room!" They both stopped and looked around to see some people actually standing there watching them.

"What the fuck! This ain't no show," Stuckey barked. The small crowd quickly scattered.

He looked at Tootsie. "Yo, you better just go use the fucking bathroom. I'ma go use this one myself. Don't fucking leave this bathroom 'til I call you out. You got that?" Stuckey's voice was soft but cruel.

"Damn, daddy, why you do me like that?"

"Don't fucking call me *daddy*. I ain't one of your tricks." He gnashed his teeth. Stuckey motioned for her to go into the bathroom. He walked into the men's restroom. He had to splash some cold water on his face and take a piss.

Tootsie walked into the bathroom pissed at Stuckey's comment. She walked over to the sink, turned on the water, and stared at it. After a minute or two, she finally had the urge to pee, and she walked into a stall. An old trick every woman knew.

She walked out of the stall and stood at the sink staring at a young lady washing her hands next to her. She watched her five foot four inch frame built like a supermodel. Her hair was long and jet-black with one streak of blue. Her skin was a light caramel color, and her eyes were gray and bright. Tootsie tried to make eye contact with her, but the stranger kept her eyes glued to her hands.

"Excuse me, but can you tell me where you got your Nudie jeans from? I've been looking for a pair for the longest," Tootsie tried to strike up a conversation with her and look into her eyes.

"Oh, I got them when I was in New York a few months back," the young lady replied as she grabbed a paper towel to dry her hands.

"I just love New York. I usually stay in Brooklyn when I'm there. You got peoples there?" Tootsie asked.

"Yeah, one of my college friends has a house out there in Park Slope. It's cool but so busy, you know what I mean?"

"Yeah, it's like that but you just got to go with the flow, you know. Do you live around here?" Tootsie was happy she was still keeping this conversation going.

"Yeah, I do. What about you?" the young lady asked.

"Actually, I just moved here with my brother and have no friends. You must think I'm nuts talking to you for this long," Tootsie lied.

"No, not at all"—she laughed and felt more relaxed— "I know how it is moving to a new place with no friends. Listen, I usually don't do this but take my number. I could show you around. If you like soul food I know a great spot," the young lady waited for Tootsie to pull out her phone.

Tootsie reached into her pocketbook pretending to search for her phone. "Oh, damn, I must of left it in the car."

"I don't got a pen, do you?"

"Damn, neither do I . . ." Tootsie stood there hoping someone would walk in.

"Well, listen, I got to go, but I work at a restaurant called All Things Good. Come by and we can talk. My name is Heaven." The young lady left, smiling at Tootsie.

As the door opened Tootsie heard her name. She washed her hands and said out loud, "All Things Good." She walked out of the bathroom door smiling.

Before they headed back to their seats, Stuckey stopped and stared Tootsie in her eyes. "Listen, Shawn P can't know nothin' 'bout what happened earlier or else I won't be the guy babysitting you."

"Stuckey, your secret is safe with me." Her lips touched his gently. "Maybe we could finish what we started and forget about this game. What do you think?"

"You see how loose you are. You get a little sniff of my attraction and you wanna take it there," Stuckey replied disappointed and started walking toward their section. He looked back at her, cutting his eyes.

Tootsie got the hint. *When this nigga around Shawn P, he ain't showing me no love,* she thought as she quickly increased her speed. *He's my way in. I gotta find out exactly what I'm doing in Detroit. Could Serenity be here? Is this it? But why put me with a babysitter? I want her dead just as bad.*

Chapter 5

Serenity walked into her bedroom with Cass on her mind. Her thought of actually being with a man was exciting. Ever since Rock died she didn't even think about men, and she definitely didn't think about women. Her feelings for women didn't disappear but were tucked away. Serenity thought if she would get involved with a guy she wouldn't feel the urge to want a woman's touch again.

Even after all the crazy shit Sadie put her through, she was grateful to her still. Sadie was a psycho bitch, but she had her good moments. Sadie knew how Serenity felt and when and how she wanted it. Rock never took time for that; he just did—shopping sprees, parties, and a little dick every once in a while if he could keep his cock hard long enough.

Serenity stared at the ceiling while lying on her bed. Her iPod was playing in her ear. Her mind kept wondering about Cass. *He was so fucking fine. Dropping my panties wouldn't be hard at all, but I ain't no ho. He gonna have to wait a little. Damn, I wish I would'a gotten his number,* she thought.

Her clit began to tingle. She placed her fingers on top of it to soothe her wet flesh. Her thoughts of Cass's hands touching her made her moan. The sounds of "Sex Me" by R. Kelly made her hot. She rubbed her clit harder and pinched on her nipple. Her back started to arch as she closed in on her climax. She wanted to feel

Cass's dick inside her. Serenity stroked her dripping wet, bald pussy faster. Her legs started to shake. She placed three fingers inside her pink slit, moving them in and out with expert precision. A surge of wetness flowed onto her fingers. She massaged the wetness all over her pussy, then put her fingers into her mouth to taste herself. "Oh damn, I got to get some dick for real," Serenity said out loud, then headed to the shower.

"Yo, Carla, you think I could borrow the car since mine is in the shop?" Serenity shouted from her room pulling on her stretch leggings by True Religion.

"I guess, but you know today is Friday, and you know how I do . . ." Carla said smiling and popping her collar up.

"It'll be quick, I promise," she continued. "I just been craving that catfish we had the other night."

Carla rushed into Serenity's bedroom, grinning. "Oh, it ain't the catfish you craving. You wanna see that dude again, don't you?"

"No, not at all. I'm going there for the food." Serenity couldn't hold back her laughter. "A'ight, you got me. I want to see if Cass is there and maybe get his number."

"Well, by the looks of things, you gonna be walking out of there with him following closely behind you like a puppy," Carla busted out, eyeing Serenity from head to toe.

"Okay, Serenity, but . . ." Carla's facial expression changed. Her face showed worry and concern. "Maybe . . . Maybe I should just tag along with you jus—"

"Oh, hell, fucking no! Since when you a cock blocker? Nope, no, and hell fucking no," Serenity cut her off. She walked to her closet searching for her wedged, open-toed Jimmy Choo sandals.

"Serenity, you don't even know this dude. Just 'cause he dished out everything for free don't mean he ain't after you for something. Please, I just don't need no shit happening to you again," Carla pleaded with Serenity.

"Carla, let's be realistic. That bitch Sadie is dead, and that crazy-ass Tootsie . . . Well, according to yo' ass, she damn near got a life sentence, so what the fuck I got to worry 'bout? It's been over a year now. I want to get on with my life without having to watch my back everywhere I go or with everyone I meet. Isn't that why we moved out of Chicago?" Serenity let out a sigh.

"Well, I don't like it," Carla replied.

"What? You don't like me getting on with my life, or you don't like me getting on with some dude?" Serenity questioned.

"Serenity, I don't give a flying fuck who you get on with, man or woman. I just want you to be safe. You the only family I got," Carla said.

"All I'm saying is let me live. I think I know the signs of a psycho. Shit, I don't even have the dude's number yet. I haven't even been on a date yet, damn!" Serenity looked at her sister and saw her eyes filled with tears. She grabbed Carla's hands. "Sis, I'm fine. Ain't no need for all this," Serenity spoke in a softer tone.

Carla hugged Serenity tightly. "I just don't want nothing to happen to you, little sis. I wouldn't know what I would do. I almost lost you once and didn't have a clue about what was going on." Carla wiped her tears away and stepped back.

"I know, sis, but I need some space. Besides, ain't nobody gonna get with me if you keep shadowing me. Now, can I get the keys to the car?" Serenity asked calmly.

"Serenity, this dude may seem all that, but trust me, he into some illegal shit too. I just don't need you caught up in somethin' like that again. 'Cause God help me, I'ma be the one going to jail or dead from tryin' to kill a nigga over you." Carla reached into her pocket and handed her the keys, then walked away.

Suddenly, her mind switched. She grabbed her phone to call some friends who could answer her questions about this Cassidy.

"Oh, shit . . . Yeah, girl, suck that big dick . . . Oh, damn . . ." Stuckey's voice bounced around the hotel room.

"Yeah, baby, I know you like it." Tootsie slowly took Stuckey's solid wood into her mouth. She teased him by rapidly moving her tongue on the tip of his shaft. She would then swallow him whole while groping his sack with her soft hands.

"Come on, let me get a taste of that pussy."

"Oh, yeah . . . Daddy, lick it . . ."

Tootsie suddenly didn't feel any heat on her clit.

"What the fuck is wrong with you? I done told you, don't ever fuckin' call me *daddy*. Stupid fuckin' bitch! I ain't no fuckin' trick! Get the fuck outta here, now!" Stuckey stood up, walked to the window naked, and shouted at her.

Tootsie tried to use her sexiest voice to lure him back to the bed. "Stuckey, I'm sorry. I'm just so used to—"

"You just so used to being a fucking ho. Now, I done told you to get the fuck up outta here. What the fuck is taking you so long?" Stuckey bawled at her again.

Tootsie felt like shit and didn't know how to respond. It was obvious he wasn't going to come back to the bed. She picked up her clothes and underwear off the floor and walked into her adjacent room with tears in her eyes.

Stuckey stood there naked with a limp noodle watching her leave. He didn't want her to leave, but he wasn't going to be called *daddy*. That was the worst thing she could do. His entire childhood life all he heard was his momma calling every man by that name. His mother didn't care about the men; she was only chasing her high. When he got older and started to hang in the streets, his reality hit him hard. His mother was a prostitute and a drug addict. He dropped out of high school and turned to the streets. He hustled enough money to send his mother to rehab so she wouldn't have to use that label again. He was finally happy and was proud to be his mother's son. After six months out of rehab, she relapsed and died from an overdose. Stuckey's world was crushed, and from that day forward, he vowed no woman he fucked with would label him *daddy*.

Chapter 6

"Iris?" Carla approached a light-skinned female at the bar.

"Yes. Hi, Carla, have a seat," Iris said, wanting to make clear that she was controlling this meeting.

"I was a little reluctant to approach because I don't remember you having blond hair."

"Oh yeah, well, change is good. So if you were reluctant to approach, what changed your mind?" Iris asked, interested in her answer.

"Do I have to say, I think it's pretty obvious? You are drop-dead gorgeous! But I didn't come here for that . . ." Carla eyed her to see if she had a chance to take it there.

Iris giggled. She knew her appearance wasn't average. "Let's talk some business. I did a little checking and know you are the one around here to make a party lively with eye candy."

Carla's eyebrows went up. *So, she checked up on me. I hope that's a good thing,* she thought.

"Okay, how would you like to get out of the drug game and get into something a little safer?" Iris asked. "It could put the same amount of, or double, the cash in your pocket."

Carla sat up straight. "I'm listening."

"I found out that you're the one who knows all the hot females in the Chicago area, and I know you not in the pimp game. It was easy to figure out that you were their supplier, not they daddy." Iris laughed, gentling nudging her with an elbow. "After all that went down with Rock, you were out of a supplier"—she raised her hand—"and please don't. I know exactly who you were contacting along the East Coast. You may not know, but I have a lot of friends all over." She winked at her.

"A'ight, so you know my game. Yeah, I was their supplier, but they also did party gigs for me too, and I would get a cut of that as well. What does that have anything to do with getting what I need?"

"I was proposing that you use your skills to acquire a few ladies to work for me." Iris motioned the bartender over to order a drink.

"What do you mean, 'work for you'? What, you a madam or somethin'?" Carla asked, almost choking on her spit.

"And what if I am? Why would you even care if I was ready to pay you ten Gs for each female you bring me?" Iris took a sip of her martini.

"Ten Gs, huh? And, exactly what do they have to do?" Carla's voice became serious. She feared where this was going.

"Well, that's my business, isn't it?" Iris spoke as if she was insulted. "If I were some nigga, you wouldn't give a fuck about what happens to 'em girls, now, would you?"

Carla's demeanor showed defeat. Her shoulders began to slouch. She knew Iris was right, because if it was any nigga in front of her, she would have been knocking shots back, celebrating their new business venture. She took a sip of her drink before she spoke. "How soon do I receive payment after gettin' the girl to you?"

"Great. We can discuss the details over breakfast in the morning. Take this . . ." she reached into her pocketbook and pulled out an envelope, then placed it on top of the bar. "It's an advance on your first girl."

"How did you know I was going to agree?" Carla took the envelope.

"I didn't, but I do know that everyone has their price. And I know you ain't got no choice 'cause your old supplier is gunnin'—I mean, no longer fucking with you and making sure no one else is too. Call me in the morning to link up. Enjoy some more drinks on me." She waved the bartender over and gave him two one-hundred-dollar bills and left the bar.

Carla watched Iris walk out without another word. She told the bartender to give her five shots of Silver Patrón immediately. After she received all five shots, she swallowed the fiery liquid just as fast. She sat there contemplating what she was getting herself into. She didn't know exactly what Iris was going to do with the girls. *I got to think about my family, Serenity. Most of 'em girls just closet crackheads and dope fiends anyway. This shit will bring me the paper a whole lot faster than me hustlin'. Fuck it, I need that money!* She ordered five more shots and told the bartender to call her a cab.

Carla came to the conclusion that once she made enough money, she would get out before it was too late and it escalated to a higher level.

Serenity walked into All Things Good and headed to the bar and asked the bartender, "Can I place a takeout order?"

"You sure can, sweetie, but can you give me like five minutes? I just gotta get these drinks out," a high-pitched voice spoke.

Serenity was taken aback. The bartender was a male and very fine. "Yeah, that's cool, but can you give me the takeout menu, and then you can take your time," she said with a smile.

The bartender handed her the menu and continued to pour drinks into glasses for the waitress. A voice spoke over the lunchtime noise, "Hey, how are things looking?"

Serenity turned around and saw a strikingly beautiful woman talking to Cass. *I wasn't really expecting him to be here. Well, like I said, my life has to start,* she thought as she grabbed a napkin to remove the sweat from her palms. She stood and walked a few steps closer, then took a deep breath. "Hey, Cass," she finally spoke.

"Oh, wow! Serenity, I was wondering when you were gonna come back," Cass smiled.

"Cass, I guess I'll talk to you later. I see I just lost your full attention," Heaven said with an attitude.

"Oh, I'm sorry. I didn't mean to interrupt, but the last time I was here I didn't get to thank Cass for his hospitality," Serenity spoke in a soft tone, not wanting any confrontation with this chick. She didn't know what kind of relationship they had.

"Forgive me, Serenity"—he motioned to Heaven—"this is my sister. She keeps everybody in check around here, including me. Why don't you have a seat at the bar and let me finish with Miss-Whip-My-Ass, and then we can talk."

"Heaven, it's nice to meet you. Cass, take your time. Business comes first." Serenity turned around and sat back at the bar.

"Damn, Heaven, why you so mean? Can't you be nice to any of the girls I like?" Cass threw his hands up in the air. "Let's just make this quick," he said, still aggravated.

"She ain't no different than the little hoes you got comin' to the lounge parties. Anyway, you got to sign some checks, and two girls have just quit. I don't have any backups that are available, so you need to get on the phone and solve it, 'cause I ain't busing no tables or bartending tonight," Heaven said with seriousness.

"Okay, let's see . . . Call the dinner hostess to come in early and help out with waiting tables and tell the hostess now to wait tables or whatever you need so that you can host. Ain't nothing you can't handle. I'll make a call and get another girl over here right away. I'll also sign the checks and put them in your office," Cass said calmly.

"Sounds good but I ain't trying to host all day and night so gets to calling whoever!" Heaven walked off toward the entrance.

Cass quickly walked over to Serenity and took a seat beside her. "Sorry about that. My sister can be a bitch sometimes."

"No need to apologize. Sometimes you need to be a bitch to get things done," Serenity offered.

"Are you?"

"Are you willing to stick around to find out?" Serenity turned the question around.

Cass looked at her and stood up. "Well, I guess that makes it official. Where would you like to get married?"

Serenity giggled and blushed. "Married? We haven't been on our first date. You don't even know me," Serenity spoke with a little suspicion.

Cass smiled and burst out laughing. "You should of saw you face!" He tried to control his laughter.

His laughter was contagious. Serenity couldn't hold back her giggles. "That is not funny. You just don't know," she said, relieved that he wasn't serious.

"I'm sorry, but I couldn't resist. But seriously, I would love to get to know you." Cass saw the takeout menu she was looking at. "Listen, I would love to have our first date now, but after the conversation I just had with my sister, you wouldn't want a second. Let's exchange numbers and we can talk to each other later. Is that possible?"

"Yes, that's possible," Serenity said with a smile.

Cass pulled out his iPhone and touched in her number. He was happy to see her. He had been asking everyone if they knew her, but no one said that they did or didn't. "Okay, so I'll talk to you later." He waved for the bartender and said to him, "Rico, make sure she gets whatever she wants and give her the dining menu not just the takeout menu. Oh yeah, and everything is on the house."

"Sure thing, Boss," Rico stated.

"Cass, you don't have to do that. I can pay my way," Serenity said a bit insulted.

"No, I insist. Besides, it would hurt my pride if you paid." Cass's tone was deep and masculine.

"Well, I guess I can get used to that." Serenity laughed. "I'll call you later and thank you."

Cass wanted to passionately kiss her, but he decided on kissing her soft hand instead. He didn't want her to feel the panties were his first objective.

Gentleman, she thought, feeling his soft lips against her skin.

She turned to Rico and took the other menu. After looking at all the entrees she decided on the barbequed chicken and house salad, along with some peach cobbler. As she waited, she looked at her phone on the bar and noticed a text from her sister. She didn't want to open it. Instantly, her nerves were on edge. Serenity thought after their big blowup she would get the hint. She didn't bother opening it; instead, she just deleted it. "Damn, can I get some fucking breathing room," Serenity mumbled in an angry tone.

"Hey . . ." a female voice spoke. "We didn't . . . Excuse me, I didn't make a good impression on you. I'm Cass's younger sister, and when things get crazy in here, I can be a bit bitchy," Heaven said, indicating that she heard her mumbling.

"Heaven, no need to explain, I know it probably can get a bit crazier than this. Besides, running this joint must be a lot of work. But it's good to see that it's a family thing," Serenity said with a friendlier tone, knowing Heaven probably saw her angry looks.

"Yeah, it's a good thing. So, if you don't mind me asking, how did you meet my brother?" Heaven asked with curiosity.

"Well, I had just moved to town from Chicago and me and my sister was starvin'. Long story short, we came here, only to find out the wait was over an hour. Your brother almost knocked me to the floor, and I guess he wanted to apologize. So, he got us a table instantly and insisted that he would take care of the bill. We had some damn good food. And, I really don't like Southern food, but I gotta give to y'all, it was slap-yo'-momma good!" Serenity rubbed her stomach.

"Well, I'm glad you liked it." Heaven tried not to stare at Serenity. Her body was perfect. Her breasts were the ideal size. Her attire was on point. She didn't have a hair out of place. Her makeup was just right.

Serenity took a sip of her homemade lemonade Rico brought her while she waited. She felt a little uncomfortable because of the pause in Heaven's conversation. She glanced at Heaven and said, "Why you staring at me like that?"

"Oh . . ." Heaven said embarrassed. "I'm sorry, but I thought you looked familiar. You ain't no model is you?"

"No, I was never a model. But you can say I was a celebrity at one point so you might have seen my picture in the paper under those party reviews and stuff." Serenity didn't want to lie, but she did.

"Yeah, you're probably right. Well, anyway, I gotta go. Hopefully, I'll see you again. It was nice meeting you." Heaven stood up and left to go to her office.

Serenity didn't know what to think. She sure as hell didn't want Heaven digging in her past to scare Cass away.

Chapter 7

"Yo, my nigga, why you ain't tell me you were coming into town. I would have set up everything. You know how I do," Cass spoke into the phone.

"Well, actually, I am here on some other shit, but I was wondering about gettin' some food delivered to my hotel. What you say?" Shawn P rubbed his stomach as he spoke.

"You ain't sayin' nothin'. Just text me the address and I'll hook you up. How long you in town?"

"That's what's up! I'm here for a minute, but I will come through soon enough. I just gotta take care of some business for the upcoming week. So, I'ma see after. Don't worry, I will settle up with you then," Shawn P replied.

"Sounds good, fam. See ya soon." Cass hung up the phone and went straight to the kitchen.

"Yo, Stuckey," Shawn P hollered as he entered Stuckey's hotel room carrying a knapsack. "Get Tootsie in here. We got some shit to settle. I don't have all day neither," Shawn ordered.

"A'ight . . ." Stuckey said uneasily. He hoped this bitch didn't blow up his spot. He took a deep breath and knocked on Tootsie's door. "Yo, get out here. Shawn wanna talk to you," Stuckey barked at the door to the adjacent room.

Tootsie entered the room and saw Shawn sitting in the lounge chair about to light a blunt.

"Both of you sit down. There's some shit about to go down. My people told me that Carla, Serenity's sister, is here in Detroit. So, that means only one thing, that Serenity is here too," he said, then inhaled the smoke from his blunt. "Tootsie, it's time you pay up for all the shit I done got you out of. You know when I came to see you and agreed to involving you it was a done deal. Basically, you owe me your life"—he paused as he took another long pull—"so you going to do what I say until this shit is done with. Now, tell me everything about this Serenity chick I don't already know."

"Ummm . . ." Tootsie stuttered.

"Don't play no games with me, bitch. You know what I want to know." Shawn's voice was sinister.

"Well, you already know that she digs females. Her sister is a minor playa in the game . . . but has some connects with some major pimps in Chi-town."

"I already know what her sister does and how she gets her money. That ain't what I'm asking you. Tell me something I don't know." Shawn's voice got louder.

"I just don't know what to tell you," Tootsie said almost in tears, fearing she would be sent back to turn tricks.

"Listen, when I spoke to you, you told me—matter of fact, you fucking *convinced* my ass—that you can get to Serenity. You know I can't get to her. And, honestly, I could get Stuckey over here to just take her out, but that's too easy. I want her to suffer in the worst kind of way. So, you better explain to me how to get her the way I want her," Shawn demanded.

"Shawn, I know you helped me and I'm grateful for that, but I can't go after Serenity myself. She would recognize me and call the police on me. Then I would surely be back in the psycho ward. I do know, however, that she took mounds of coke and weed. She didn't drink all that much. Most of all, she loved to have sex with women no matter how much she denied it," Tootsie's voice trembled.

"Well, then, that's the angle we gonna have to go with. I want that bitch to pay. It may take a minute, but in the end, I'm gonna get that ass. Tootsie, I want you to write down every type of female she liked and use this"—he pulled out a laptop from his knapsack—"to connect with her through Facebook, Twitter, and any other social networks they got out these days. Hopefully, she stupid enough to fall into the setup. Tootsie, once she comfortable with you, try to get her to meet you, and then we can shut the bitch down for good," Shawn said.

"Okay, I'll just pull a pic of some random chick and try to connect with her. Um, do you think we could go somewhere to eat 'cause this takeout food ain't working. And, Stuckey won't take me nowhere," Tootsie whined.

"Ah, stop your fuckin' bitching. Take this card and order some food. You can look up their menu online. Now, you can go back to your room and tell Stuckey once you make a connection," he said annoyed.

"All Things Good?" Her eyebrows arched. "Can I get a phone?" she quickly asked.

"Right, well, I may fix that if you come up with something good. Just remember what we talked about. This is where you show me your gratitude."

Tootsie grabbed the laptop and stood to head to her room. She was relieved that she wasn't here to turn tricks, but getting Serenity involved with some random chick would be hard. She had to figure a way out of this death trap Shawn was setting her ass up for. Tootsie sat on her bed and powered the laptop on. She was so excited to get something more than just TV and Stuckey's dull company. She had no phone but having a laptop was the next best thing. She typed on the keyboard and found what she was looking for—Heaven. Tootsie smiled and sent a friend request through Facebook.

"Stuckey, you okay? You look worried. What's up?" Shawn questioned.

"Nah, boss, I ain't worried, but I just didn't think I would be here for another couple of months, that's all," Stuckey said.

"Put it this way. You ain't hustlin' in the street to get locked up. That's why I placed you with her. I know I could trust you. I know you wouldn't fall for her games. She's a conniving bitch, trust me," Shawn said, passing Stuckey a fresh blunt and the knapsack.

Stuckey looked into the bag and saw wads of cash. A smile spread across his face immediately. "You right about that shit."

"You down for this, right?" Shawn asked, seeking assurance.

"Yeah, I'm down, but exactly how much money you tryin' to give a bro?" Stuckey answered with a question.

"Put it this way. If shit work out, your cut may just make you leave the game altogether. And I would be fine with that. Stuckey, I trust you unconditionally and wouldn't play you," Shawn said, taking the blunt from him.

"I know that. We go way back, and you schooled me when I was a novice. So, whatever you need to do, I got your back," Stuckey spoke sincerely.

"Good, now let's talk about this bitch here," Shawn said while motioning to the adjacent room.

"What about her? I been keepin' her out of sight, out of mind, know what I mean? That's why it tripped me out when you came through with 'em tickets for the game."

"Yeah, it probably tripped her ass out too. But that's the thing. I need this bitch happy, but I need her to know that I'm behind all that. It's a mental thing with these bitches. You see, I put her ass in a low place in D.C., and now that she's here in Detroit, she gonna live better 'cause of me." Shawn continued with his explanations and plan. "Listen, I still want you to keep her on the low, but let her breathe sometimes. You know, leave the keys around, leave your phone around, then leave for like twenty minutes or so. Then, when you come back, check things out, make sure she ain't calling no one and shit like that.

"That laptop she got"—his voice became lower, and Stuckey moved closer to hear his every word—"I got someone to put some shit on there so when I look at my laptop I know every key she hits. I gotta make sure that bitch ain't gonna do no stupid shit."

"A'ight, then, what if she leaves? Then what?" Stuckey asked, wanting to know his true intentions.

"Make her sleep with 'em fishes in Lake Erie! Don't worry, this ain't gonna last for long. I got some other plans in the makin'." Shawn P stood up and left.

Stuckey sat there looking at the money in the bag. Finally, he stood and took the bag to the table, emptied the money out, and counted out $50,000. He watched the adjacent room door and before he could act on putting the money away, a whiff of chronic caught his nose. Stuckey pulled out a quarter pound of White Widow chronic. He moved swiftly and pulled some weed out of the ziplock bag to set it on the table. "I'ma smoke that right now," he said in a whisper. He closed the ziplock, grabbed the money, and went to the safe in the closet of his room. He returned smiling with a fresh Dutch Master in his hand and was surprised to see Tootsie sitting with the laptop at the table.

"What you doing in here?"

"I could smell that weed from my room. You think I could smoke with you? I haven't hit a blunt since I been here," Tootsie spoke in her softest voice, hoping he wouldn't dismiss her. She needed to get on his good side. She wanted to know what Shawn P had planned for her. She had to find a way into his head.

"Yeah, a'ight," Stuckey replied, remembering Shawn's words. He watched as she planted her phat ass on the sofa with shorts barely covering her ass cheeks.

Cass looked at his watch and noticed it was already eight o'clock and Serenity still hadn't called him. *Maybe, I should call her . . . I'll send her a text just sayin' hello,* Cass thought as he keyed Hello into his iPhone. Five minutes later he read her reply.

How u? Busy?

Cass replied back, Good. Yes. Just sayin' hello.

That's a good thing. Call me when it dies down a bit, Serenity's words flashed across the screen.

I will. It could be real late, okay?

Anytime, it doesn't matter.

Before Cass could put his phone in his pocket it vibrated in his hand. "Hey, everything good? How was that catfish I sent you?"

"Oh man, that shit made me wanna smack somebody! It was off the muthafuckin' chain, man! But listen, I need another favor . . . There will be a young lady calling in for some deliveries, and I need for you to make that happen. Can you set that up?" Shawn asked, not indicating any other details.

"Shawn, listen, you know you my dude, but this place here ain't no delivery service. I make that exception for you. I don't know, Shawn . . ." Cass's voice showed he wasn't happy about the request.

"Cass, you don't have to go to the extent of what you do for me. It could be something little just every once in a while, then something real good. I *will* make it worth your while, though," Shawn threw in an incentive.

"Yeah, a'ight, but you gonna have to give me some money up front. When can you come down here?" Cass hated to pass up easy money.

"I could make a stop by the end of the week. Would five Gs hold you for a while?" Shawn didn't want to give up any more money than he had to.

"Make it six and we have a deal."

Shawn laughed. "Cass, you always after that money. Yeah, a'ight. Six. I'll text you the details on who will be callin' in, and you'll have your money tomorrow. I'ma gonna drop off the money tomorrow." Shawn P promised, then hung up the phone.

What does this nigga think—I run a fast-food joint or something? Cass thought.

"So, did you find out if she on that Facebook bullshit?" Stuckey asked as he blew smoke into the air and passed the blunt to Tootsie.

"I found her, but she ain't accepting none of my friend requests. But don't worry. I'ma get through. Maybe I gotta try a different picture," Tootsie said.

"I'm sure you'll come up with somethin', but don't even think 'bout sendin' her your picture," Stuckey said.

"You know what I need . . . a camera. Yeah, I could use that," she blew smoke out into the air.

"A camera, huh? You know you can't be takin' no pictures. What the fuck do you think this is?" Stuckey asked, concerned that she would blow everything.

"Don't get tight, nigga. I ain't gonna be takin' no pictures of yo' ass, trust me," Tootsie assured him.

"Well, you better not be or shit ain't gonna be sweet once Shawn find out 'bout it. So you better not do nothin' stupid," he reminded her.

Stuckey sat back in a daze from the trees he just smoked with Tootsie. He watched her as she typed away on the laptop. His dick started to rise. He needed some release. Stuckey thought carefully. *Well, if I dick her down good enough, she ain't gonna leave and my babysitting will become much easier. Besides, I ain't hit nothin' in a minute!*

Tootsie peeked at Stuckey and could see his buddy making an appearance. *This could be the only thing I can do to get into Shawn P's head,* she thought. She stopped typing on the computer and walked over to Stuckey. She got on her knees. She said a silent prayer that he wouldn't knock her ass down. His sweatpants gave him away. Stuckey's dick was standing tall and visible. She smiled, then pulled his sweats down to his ankles. Then she devoured his cock. She worked her deep-throat magic and heard him moaning. When she glanced at his face, she was happy to see he was pleased.

"You like it, Stuckey? You like how I suck you?"

"Ow, you know I do . . . fuck . . . Yeah, suck this big dick . . ." Stuckey screamed out, then abruptly stood up. "Now, suck it!" he moaned, grabbing her head and attempting to ram his dick into the back of her throat.

"Yeah . . . Stuckey, I want you in me right now," Tootsie quickly said, covering up that she almost called him *daddy.* She stood up and pushed him onto the small sofa. Quickly, she turned around so her ass was in view while she bounced on his thick rod.

"Ow . . . yeah, baby . . . Jiggle that ass . . ." Stuckey slapped her ass.

Tootsie bounced harder on his dick as he continued to slap her round phat ass. "Yeah, baby, you like that . . ."

Stuckey grabbed her closely and picked her up with his cock still in her wet pussy. Her face hit the cushions of the sofa with her ass in the air. He pushed his tool deep inside her as he positioned her body on the sofa. He pumped hard and deep into her flesh for many minutes. Just when he was about to climax, he quickly brought her face to his erupting dick.

The warm, sticky liquid was covering Tootsie's mouth. She opened her mouth, and his jimmy was sucked again until he reached another climax. Tootsie dug deep into her bag of tricks to make him cum again in less than five minutes. Stuckey almost fell to his knees, they were so weak. Covered with sweat, he quickly took a seat on the sofa.

"Damn, girl, what you tryin' to do to a nigga? Fuck!" Stuckey said out of breath.

"I like you, that's all," Tootsie said rising from the sofa.

"Where you going?" Stuckey asked.

"I'm going to my room to take a shower. You want me to come back?" Tootsie hoped he would.

"Oh, a'ight. Yeah, we can hit another blunt when you come back," Stuckey said.

Tootsie walked into her room and shut the door behind her. She ran to the bathroom and hovered over the toilet bowl. Her stomach felt nauseated. She felt her mouth watering and spit into the toilet. Before she knew it, her lunch was no longer in her stomach. It was floating in front of her eyes. She kneeled in front of the porcelain god and tried to stop her head from spinning. Then she slowly stood up and went to the sink. She turned on the cold water and splashed it against her face. *I gotta get myself together,* she thought as she shook herself. Right after that, she got into the shower and got back her stability. Then she dressed quickly, fearing that Stuckey would forget about his invitation.

Stuckey stood in his room fresh out of the shower, laughing along with the TV. He went to the nightstand and picked up a hefty amount of weed and walked out of the room. He grabbed the Dutch and spilt it like a master. Then he dumped the contents of the cigar into the garbage bin next to the table. Afterward, he took a seat and started to crush the weed with his fingers over the tobacco leaf. Before he finished licking the Dutch Master into perfect form, Tootsie walked in, wearing only a tight red tank top with matching G-string. Her hair was perfectly be-weavable. He knew it wasn't hers, because it didn't even get frizzy with all that sweat they produced earlier.

"Is it okay if I come in?" Tootsie asked.

"Why you ask that? I already told you it was cool," he said, trying to keep himself from not jumping into her hot flesh once again.

"'Cause the way you lookin' at me, like you ain't seen me before, that's all."

"Nah, it ain't that. So, you ready to smoke?" Stuckey held the newly rolled blunt in the air.

"Sure am. You wanna see what's on TV? Maybe we could order some movie or somethin'," she said.

Stuckey put fire to one end of the blunt and inhaled deeply. "That's a plan."

Chapter 8

A week went by since Tootsie received the laptop from Shawn P. It was early that morning when she heard Stuckey shuffling around in the room next to hers. She picked up the box of Newports on the nightstand next to the bed, reached for her lighter, and sparked one up. Then she sat up in bed wondering how stupid Stuckey was. After their first encounter, she figured the only way to get into his head was by putting it on him in the worst way. Since then, he was indeed hooked.

She heard the middle door to enter Stuckey's room close shut and a lock clicking. Tootsie knew he would be gone for a minute. She reached for the laptop on the nightstand, logged onto her Facebook account, and found her friend request alert was blinking.

Your friend request has been accepted. You are now friends with Heaven.

She smiled from ear to ear. Tootsie immediately clicked on Heaven's file. She's a Cancer, single, loves Urban Books, and totally gorgeous all-around. When she first met Heaven at the football game she didn't expect to see her again. Tootsie's luck finally changed. She looked at all her pictures which were mostly the celebrity dinner parties held at a restaurant. Tootsie didn't care about any of that; her main focus was getting Heaven into her bed or anything close to that.

Tootsie looked at her screen to see if Heaven was online to chat, and she was.

Hello? Tootsie typed, hoping she would answer.

There was no reply. Ten minutes went by and still no reply. Tootsie didn't want to scare her so she typed again.

Hello? I don't know if u remember, but I met u at the game in the bathroom.

Tootsie waited patiently and within minutes Heaven finally replied.

Oh, right . . . how did u find me?

Tootsie smiled looking at the screen. *I gotta see where her head at*, she thought before she typed.

I remembered when u said u worked 4 All Things Good. The food is outstanding BTW.

Tootsie's palms started to sweat. She quickly ran into the bathroom and washed her hands and smoothed her hair into a loose ponytail. When she returned, Heaven had already sent two replies.

Thanks. Yeah, that's right. U asked me 'bout my Nudie jeans. How come I ain't see u? Did you get takeout? So where u stayin'?

Tootsie looked at the screen and read her response out loud, then paused. "Well, that was expected." She didn't want Heaven to think she was baiting her or some kind of weird stalker chick.

I'm here with my boyfriend on some business. And I'm bored as hell!!

A few minutes went by before Heaven's words appeared.

Oh, that's cool. So u should come by and get a drink. I'm always here!

Tootsie knew exactly what to type. She only hoped that her response would be good enough.

Well, ain't nothin' wrong with hard work . . . But I gotta b honest with u. My boyfriend ain't so cool when it comes 2 me goin' out, if u know what I mean.

Heaven responded with a surprising question.

Damn, girl, why u do that 2 urself? I don't mean 2 b all in ur business, and I definitely don't want no drama.

Tootsie didn't expect her next reply.

Listen, I'ma keep it simple. I don't want no friendship. I saw the way u looked at me. I know u was just frontin'. U liked what u saw, correct?

Tootsie's jaw dropped as she read. She didn't know how she lucked up, but she did. She reached for another cigarette and lit it. *Damn, this can't be*, she thought before she responded.

Yeah, u right. Those jeans made ur ass look real good. Since u want 2 b simple, I'm just lookin' 4 fun. I don't want 2 meet. I don't want 2 talk 2 u on the phone. If I want 2 talk 2 u, I rather video chat so I can watch u rub that pussy.

Tootsie's juices were starting to flow by how sudden her chat with Heaven was evolving into something so good. She pulled off her tank top and rubbed her nipples until they were hard. She pushed a few keys of the keyboard, then sat on her heels and caressed her breasts while puckering her lips toward the laptop. A flash went off. She changed her position. She lay on the bed exposing her round ass through her black lace boy short cut underwear. She pushed some more keys and a flash of light was seen again. Tootsie quickly sent them to Heaven and asked if she wanted to play.

U look so good. I can't play. I gotta go 2 work. But stay logged in. Maybe I can lock myself in the office and play with u 4 a minute.

Before Tootsie could reply, her conversation with Heaven was deleted and another message box popped open.

Bitch, who the fuck u think u talkin' 2? U suppose 2 b doin' somethin' else!

Tootsie quickly jumped off the bed, grabbed her tank top, and pulled it over her head. She ran to the door and put her ear to it. Silence. She heard nothing. She ran over to the middle door and put her ear to it. Again she heard nothing. *Who the fuck is that?* the thought went through her mind. She shook her body as if to shake a chill off her shoulders. Then she slowly approached the bed and sat in front of the computer. She looked at the username. "Watchin' u, bitch," she read out loud. *Oh my God, who the fuck . . .* before she could finish her thought, another message appeared.

Yeah, bitch, it's me. Did u actually think I was jus' gonna hand u a laptop so u can use that shit freely? U better jus' get 2 doin' what I told u n stop fuckin' 'round!

Tootsie shook her head yes as if Shawn were standing before her. The message box disappeared. She closed the laptop quickly. Tootsie took a deep breath and exhaled as thoughts jumped into her head. *I'm so fuckin' stupid. Did I really think I was gonna use this shit like it was my own? I'm trippin'! I'm sure if he can see what I'm typing, then he can definitely see what I'm doin'! Shit!*

Tootsie sat on her bed staring at the laptop, fearing to open it. She didn't want to open it thinking he would be spying on her. Tootsie knew from back in the days of hanging with Sadie that Shawn P wasn't easily tricked. She had to think. Tootsie wanted Shawn P to know who was really in control of her.

Chapter 9

A month had passed and Serenity and Cass seemed steady. They saw each other almost every day, and she ate dinner out with him on some nights. She also noticed that Carla got the hint about her needing her space. She was finally living her life, and she loved it. She even became friends with Cass's sister, Heaven, and they often went shopping together. Serenity's life was finally stable and real. She was taking some classes here and there, working part time, and most of all, she was seeing a man that excited her in every way.

Cass enjoyed Serenity's company. She was down-to-earth and didn't try too hard to come at him like the other thirsty chicks hungry for his riches. Most of his emotions about her were hung up on Serenity not allowing him to dig her back out. He wasn't about to stop either; she was too sweet to not try.

Serenity took her favorite seat at the bar and waited for Cass so they could head out for the night. Rico placed a glass of homemade lemonade in front of her. After weeks of seeing her face, he realized she didn't drink.

"Hey, chica, what's going on?" Heaven walked up to her and kissed her on her cheek.

"Oh, you know, waiting for your brother," Serenity said noticing Heaven's huge smile. "What's up with you? You sure look happy; you must of got some last night," Serenity joked.

"No, silly, but I think your plans will be changing tonight. I think you gonna be sticking around here for a while. Oh, here he comes. I'll let him tell you," Heaven motioned toward her brother who was quickly approaching.

Cass reached the bar slightly out of breath. He tried to hide his excitement. "Baby, how would you like to meet Eminem and D12?"

"Damn, Cass, you must really like his music 'cause you damn near drooling," Heaven chimed in.

Serenity laughed because he really was drooling. "Okay, Cass, you can calm down now," Serenity spoke slowly, teasing him.

"Ha-ha, very funny. You just don't know how much exposure this can bring. I already got people sending blast e-mails and postings on message boards, Facebook, MySpace, you name it. Everyone in Detroit and neighboring cities is gonna be tryin' to get in here tonight," he said with passion.

"All right, Cass, so you better start making those phone calls for added security, waitresses, and bartenders. I have the VIP guest dining area already set up. The rest is up to you," Heaven directed his attention to the work still needing to be handled.

"I know. I gotta round everyone up and put them on their A-game, 'cause shit ain't goin' to blow up in my face!" Cass kissed Serenity on the lips and ran off to alert the staff.

"All right, so now I got like a good two, three hours to kill," Heaven stated to Serenity.

"Well, I guess I got some company 'til the big entrance of these rap superstars," Serenity laughed, picking up her drink.

"Well, I better grab one of those before my big night," Heaven said, walking behind the bar. She searched for her favorite bottle of wine.

"Pinot Grigio, huh?"

"Yup, let's take this back to my office," Heaven suggested.

"Don't forget your glass and a bottle opener," Serenity reminded her.

"Don't need it, got one in my office," she laughed as she walked toward her office with Serenity following behind her.

Heaven entered her office with bottle in hand and closed the door after Serenity entered. She went straight to her desk, opened a drawer and pulled out a wineglass and a bottle opener. Heaven quickly unwrapped the soft metal covering the cork opening. She inserted the bottle opener and tried to pull the cork out easily. The difficulty made her frustrated.

Serenity saw her aggravation and laughed at her, almost spilling her drink onto her lap. "Girl, that look ain't good. Let me help you with that," Serenity continued to laugh and walked closer to her. She placed her hands on the bottle to hold it steady while Heaven pulled the cork out.

"Stop laughing, this is serious." Heaven felt a release and heard a pop.

"Heaven, you funny as hell." Serenity pushed her lightly on the shoulder.

Heaven poured herself a well-deserved glass of wine and sipped it carefully. She didn't want any to spill after all that trouble of opening it. She took a seat on her desk facing Serenity.

Serenity looked at Heaven and saw a beautiful woman and wondered why she hadn't seen her with any guy. Her blouse was tight and cut low. Her cleavage was in full view. Serenity tried to shake her thoughts of Heaven spreading her legs across the desk and her licking every inch of that sweet, pink flesh. Since hanging around

Heaven she saw little hints of her curiosity but didn't want to ask, thinking she could be insulted.

Heaven sipped her wine while she told Serenity about her plans for her upcoming trip to New York.

Serenity zoned out and paid more attention to her juicy thighs in her short-ass skirt. She didn't know why these feelings were going through her mind. Her thoughts were racing. *Why the fuck am I feeling this way? I left that behavior in the past. I can't even think of doing this . . . She's his sister. Oh my God, she's so beautiful my eyes can't stay off her!*

Heaven poured more wine into her glass. After finishing it, she leaned back trying to toss the bottle into the garbage can behind her desk. Serenity could see what was about to happen.

"Wha-o," Heaven yelled out.

Serenity stood up to reach for her quickly, preventing Heaven from rolling off the side of her desk.

Heaven instinctively grabbed Serenity closer to her. They were now face-to-face.

Serenity closed her eyes and kissed her lips softly, hoping she would reciprocate.

Heaven's panties were instantly wet. She didn't want Serenity to stop. After seeing her around so often, Heaven longed for this to happen and, until now, she only had hints about it. When they went shopping together, after awhile, they would try on clothes in front of each other, exposing every inch of their skin. Her juices flowed, and she kissed Serenity back with lust guiding her tongue.

Serenity invited Heaven's yearning desires and parted Heaven's legs a bit with her hand. She inched up and pulled her panties to the side, revealing her wet pussy. Slowly, she guided her fingers over Heaven's soft, inviting opening.

Heaven began to moan slightly and whispered, "We shouldn't be doin' this . . . ummm . . ."

"I know . . . but you feel so good . . ." Serenity didn't want to stop. She wanted to test herself. Her urges took over.

She took her other hand and unbuttoned Heaven's blouse, revealing her plump titties. Without delay, she pulled down the bra revealing her hard nipples. Serenity licked around her hard twin mounds while working the insides of her pussy with eager fingers. She could feel Heaven's legs begin to tremble. Serenity worked her thumb on Heaven's clit while her fingers moved in and out of her opening.

"Oh, keep it there . . . Serenity . . ." Heaven whispered.

Serenity licked on Heaven's neck and moved up to her lips. "Heaven . . . Can I taste it?" she asked between hot kisses.

"Are you sure? Shouldn't we stop? Do you want to take it that far? What if my brother walks in?" Heaven spit out faster than a bullet.

Serenity continued to play with the silky liquid flowing on her fingers. "It could just be our little . . . Heaven, I know the way you look at me. You want it just as bad as I do, so I think it's time to act on it and really see if we want this." Her breathing became heavy as she continued to please Heaven.

Heaven spread her legs wider, and Serenity's fingers probed deeper.

Serenity pulled Heaven's skirt up and slipped her panties off. Heaven spread her legs and cooed as Serenity's tongue touched her swollen, aching clit. She moved her tongue back and forth and sucked Heaven's bald pussy. Serenity could hear Heaven reaching her peak.

"Oh . . . yes . . . Please, don't stop . . . Suck it, Serenity
. . . yes, baby . . . I'm gonna cum." Heaven's moans were
getting louder.

Serenity quickly covered Heaven's mouth to muffle
her sounds. She moved her tongue faster over her
throbbing clit and placed three fingers deep inside her.

"Ahhh . . ." Heaven clutched Serenity's head, while
pressing her face hard between her quivering legs.

Serenity licked her flowing nectar slowly, allowing
her miniorgasm to spill over into her mouth.

Heaven's body was now on cloud nine. All she wanted
to do was lie next to Serenity and explore every inch of
her body. Heaven jumped up almost kicking Serenity
when she heard her office phone ring. In a split second,
she looked at the door and answered the phone, "Hello?"

"Heaven, can you stop bullshittin' with Serenity and
get the fuck out here? This shit has to be right. You
know what I mean?" Cass spoke into his cell.

"Okay, I'll be there shortly," Heaven said in her calm-
est voice. She waited for a response but could hear her
brother talking to the chef. She was relieved to know he
was in the kitchen all the way in the basement. She had
time, but her movements had to be fast. She hung up the
phone knowing he wouldn't care.

"Serenity, we gots to move swiftly"—she kissed her
lips. "Cass could come this way!" Heaven buttoned her
blouse and fixed her disheveled look.

"Oh, shit, Heaven!" Serenity ran into the bathroom
in the office and washed her face, then applied some
light makeup.

Serenity looked Heaven over and tamed a loose strand
of hair lingering over her eye.

Heaven looked at Serenity. "Just perfect. Now let's
go before . . ."

As Heaven opened the door, Rico was standing there just about to knock.

"Rico, shit, you scared me! What the fuck!" Heaven hoped he wasn't standing there long.

"Sorry, Heaven, but Cass called me and said to get extra cash from your office for the till tonight," Rico said, explaining his appearance.

"Oh, okay, well, there's a thousand dollars in various bills on my desk. Just go in and grab it," Heaven said, itching to get out of his face.

Serenity nudged Heaven to move forward and head out to the lounge.

"Okay, no problem. I'll lock it when I leave," Rico assured her.

Heaven headed down the short hall with Serenity whispering behind her, "You sure about that? He won't take nothin', will he?"

"Nah, he's my number-one employee. There's no funny business with him when it comes to his job. His personal life, well, that's a whole other story," Heaven said confidently.

Rico walked into the room and detected a sweet smell. He searched the desk for the money, but it wasn't there. He looked on the floor in front of her desk and still didn't see it. He moved envelopes, invoices, some more paperwork, and it wasn't there. He walked behind the desk and looked under it. What he discovered was a black laced thong on top of the stack of money. *That's why they were so thrown off by me at the door. I knew it! I knew Heaven was gay.* His thoughts of finding out his boss was gay were gratifying. He finally could speak freely about his personal life without offending her.

Rico grabbed the money and placed the thong on her chair and pushed her chair in. He wanted to let her know he knew of her little episode. He was no dummy, and blackmail is a bitch when negotiating a rise. *This way, maybe I won't have to work so hard and still have cash rolling in, at least until she comes outta that closet!* Rico snapped his fingers, pleased about his new discovery.

Chapter 10

A spanking new Continental Supersports Convertible ISR pulled to the front of the restaurant, followed by a Maserati GranTurismo S and two top-of-the-line Benzes. Cass rushed to the front of the restaurant to greet his special guests and guide them through to the VIP area. He didn't have any trouble getting through the now-growing crowd because his security did their job. He walked through with pride and saw Heaven standing in front of the VIP area. She introduced herself as they took their seats. They were all smiles.

"Now, let's get some of this food I been hearing about," someone from the entourage spoke loudly.

"No problem. I got the chef working on somethin' as we speak. Is anyone allergic to anything?" Cass asked.

"Nope," they all said in unison.

"Okay, well, you guys enjoy and please don't hesitate to ask any of the waitresses here for anything," Cass said before leaving the room with Heaven following behind him.

Heaven stopped in front of the entrance and whispered in the security guard's ear, "No one gets in or out but the waitresses. If our guests want to take their party to the lounge area, call me immediately."

Serenity sat at the bar watching Cass and Heaven do their thing. Her thoughts swirled around her head like a category-four hurricane. *What the fuck did I just do? My God, I thought my feelings were over. I'm the one who initiated the entire thing. What the fuck is wrong with me? But I liked it. I wanted it badly!* She was interrupted when Rico tapped her hand.

"You want a drink?" Rico asked, leaning closer to her.

"Nah, I'm good. I think I'm gonna leave," Serenity answered.

"Why? This place is about to be jumpin' in a hot minute," he shouted. "Who knows you might just get some . . ." Rico lowered his voice.

"What?" Serenity couldn't hear him over the noise in the dining area. She turned the stool around and stood up. She could see Cass walking toward her and Heaven heading to the lounge area.

"Hey, baby, you not leaving, right? The night is just beginning," Cass said, opening his arms for a hug and a kiss.

"Baby, I think I'm going home. This ain't my kinda thing, you know that. This growing crowd only scares me," Serenity voiced sweetly.

"Oh, I see. So, you sayin' you don't feel safe?" Cass raised his eyebrows.

"No, nothing like that. I would rather be home, that's all. Besides, I got some reading to catch up with." Serenity assured him everything was fine.

Cass kissed her lips gently. "All right, but let me get someone to walk you to your car, okay?"

"Yeah, that might be a good idea," she agreed.

He pulled out his iPhone and spoke briefly into it. Three minutes later, Serenity was being escorted out the back exit to her car by a six foot four giant. He reminded her of Michael Clarke Duncan, the actor from *The Green Mile*. She safely reached her car, and he waited for her to drive off.

***

Shawn P saw all the expensive cars that lined the block. He was impressed and definitely would have to give his props to Cass. There was a line around the block trying to get into the place.

"Damn, what the fuck! Everybody and they momma tryin' to party over here tonight," Stuckey said, looking at the expanding crowd.

"Yeah, you better park this shit in the lot over there. Let's just hope it ain't filled up already," Shawn P suggested.

Stuckey pulled into the lot, hopped out of the car, and took the ticket from the attendant. "Yo, keep that shit close by." Stuckey handed him a crisp fifty-dollar bill and walked out of the parking garage.

They both walked past the crowd to the front entrance. Females were shouting for the two men to take them in with them and what they would do if they did. Stuckey and Shawn laughed at all their suggestions and promises. They approached a six foot five male dressed in a well-stitched Brooks Brothers suit.

"Shawn P and guest. I'm sure my name is on the list," Shawn P spoke.

The man looked at a clipboard and said, "Enjoy your night."

Upon entering, Shawn P scanned the room for any not-so-friendly invitees. He rubbed his eyes and turned around to face Stuckey. "Yo, our luck done happened. Look straight-ahead by the bar."

"Oh, wow! Ain't that the bitch there talkin' to your boy, Mr.-Ready-to-Please? You can see the drool drippin' from his grill when he talkin' to her," Stuckey laughed.

"Hell, this is sweet! Our plans have changed," Shawn said, smiling at the crowd.

"It looks like she leavin'. She got some dude walking her out of the back exit," Stuckey spoke her every move.

"A'ight, Stuckey. I think your time in Detroit will be ending soon. I just hope he ain't already knee-deep in it. You know what I mean?" Shawn turned around to see her stepping out of the exit.

"Yeah, pussy can definitely get you in a situation," Stuckey added, not realizing the impact of his words.

"Go get the car and follow that bitch. Now I can go feel this nigga out," Shawn barked at him.

Stuckey moved quickly to follow Shawn's direct order.

Stuckey sat in the rental on a quiet tree-lined block. He saw Serenity walk into the house. He pulled out his phone and texted Shawn P.

I know where she stay.

Stuckey's phone vibrated.

I want u Stuckey. I'm playing with my pussy n u not here 2 watch.

He looked at the message on his screen and saw there was a picture attached to it. He saw two fingers spreading apart a pair of wet lips of a phat pink pussy. Her clit was fully visible. His dick jumped, knowing who the sender was. He dialed the hotel number and requested to be patched through to her room. He spoke softly into the phone. "You want me to stick tongue in that hole, baby . . .?" He massaged his crotch.

"No, I want somethin' stiff and big . . . You coming in soon? It's so wet, Stuckey," Tootsie teased.

"Ow, baby, just hold off. I'ma get there soon enough to stick my big, black dick in your wet, sweet pussy."

"I can't wait. You better strip once you hit the door," Tootsie said in her sexiest voice and hung up the phone. Stuckey held on to his dick and looked around. He saw that no one was coming or going so he whipped out his cock and jerked off to Tootsie's naked pictures she sent. She'd been feeding him her pussy day and night, whenever and wherever since that first time. His mind was slipping on what she was really there for.

Cass's face beamed as he walked through his lounge. Everyone was enjoying themselves, and his rap superstar guests were happy, bumping to the music with some high-priced hoes. He noticed Shawn P standing in front of the bar not bumping to the newest hit from Jay-Z. He walked over to him. "Yo, you good?"

"Yeah, man. This shit is live! I can't get over the crowd still tryin' to get in," Shawn stroked his ego.

"Yeah, that shit is bonkers out there. We got like an hour left before I have to shut this place down. I don't need no tickets from the boys in blue, know what I mean?" Cass bopped his head to the beat of the music.

"Yo, your girl must be pissed at you with shit like this poppin' off. And, you know it will only get worse with the exposure you gonna get tonight. You might need to buy the lot next door and expand this lounge area," Shawn offered some advice.

"Nah, nah, Serenity ain't big on crowds, so she don't care. But you right about expanding. I'm only allowed a max of 116 people in this area," Cass stated as he panned the room.

Shawn P knew that Cass didn't do his homework on his little girlfriend and knew nothing of his connection with her. He didn't want to press him with questions about Serenity so he just leaned back against the bar and pretended he was enjoying the music. In reality, he was thinking hard about how he was gonna get Cass to give up Serenity for good and how much money he would have to part with to make it happen.

Chapter 11

It was a Monday night, and Iris seated herself in the far back corner table in perfect view of all entrances into the restaurant. She rested her bag on the chair next to her. It was her third trip to Detroit from D.C. for the month. She loved the money she was making, so she didn't care about how many trips she had to make. As long as Carla and Cass kept the girls coming, her retirement fund was building by the day. She had almost a quarter of a million dollars stashed from their business alone. She wasn't even counting the twenty Gs a month she was getting with her drug connects.

The waitress came over to take her order.

"Can I just have the peach cobbler with a scoop of vanilla ice cream, please?" Iris asked her and handed her back the menu.

She could see Cass walking toward her table with a smile.

"Hey, lady," he said, kissing her on her cheek.

"Hello, Cass, you seem to be in a good mood," Iris commented.

"Why shouldn't I be? I'm in the presence of someone far greater than I," Cass laid the compliment on thick.

"Come on, Cass, you know flattery will get you nowhere with me," Iris's tone was cold. She looked at the bar and could see a beautiful woman standing there with her arms folded.

"Okay, then, I guess business it is," Cass said a little disappointed.

"Who's that at the bar, Cass? She look like she about to let into your bartender. I ain't never seen her sexy figure around here before. Don't tell me you keeping all the hot chicks for this place?" Iris continued to stare at Heaven.

Cass turned around to see his sister behind the bar with Rico. He turned to face Iris and said, "That's my sister. She always gettin' into somebody ass about something." Cass thought nothing of it at first, but then, it hit him like a ton of bricks. "Iris, my sister is not yours, or anybody else's, prospect, you hear me? If anything happens to my sister, Ir—"

"Calm the fuck down. Remember where you at and what you do. Ain't nobody touchin' your sister. Just fuckin' relax!" Iris reached into her bag and pulled out an envelope containing thirty Gs of crisp one-hundred-dollar bills and handed it to him. Money always makes people's mood change.

Cass took the money and slipped it into the inside pocket of his blazer. "Thank you, very much. This feels fatter than usual." His tone showed how quickly his temper switched gears.

"Yeah, it is. Let's just say the last two girls you sent my way came with a bonus," Iris replied with a smile. "So listen, I'm leaving in the morning. Did you get any girls off the bus depot?"

"I'm working on that. It's a prime location, and you should know that some of these pimps would cut you and gut you if they knew how we were getting our paper at spots. I ain't tryin' to step on anybody toes. Just give me a couple of days and I should have at least two to send to Gary," Cass assured her.

"Good, 'cause I just got another request for two more heading to Mexico," Iris showed her pearly whites.

His thoughts of his sister being in the clutches of Iris scared him. He knew exactly what happened to the girls when they got picked up from Gary. He knew their future was hopeless. Sometimes his morals would make him feel bad, but his greed for the money suppressed it well. Cass's phone sounded. He excused himself from the table and waved her a good-bye.

At the same time, the waitress brought out her order. Iris stopped the waitress from setting the plate down in front of her. "I changed my mind. This kind of treat will increase my size by the mouthful. I'm sorry, but please take this and enjoy the rest of your day." Iris reached into her purse to retrieve a hundred-dollar bill. She looked at the time on her watch. *Looks like I'm gonna be late meeting up with this chick,* she thought, walking out to hail a cab.

"Wow, thanks, Miss. You have a good day too," the waitress said with gratitude.

Carla awoke from her afternoon nap and waltzed into the kitchen for some water. She noticed Serenity reading the latest release from Carl Weber on the sofa as she walked by. Carla returned to the living room with a glass of water in her hands. "Good book?" she asked Serenity.

"Hmm . . ." Serenity continued reading as if a question were not posed to her.

"Okay, I guess it must be good 'cause your ass ain't even look up," Carla spoke out loud, knowing Serenity wasn't paying her no mind. "What's up with you? Like you don't talk to me no more. What, am I not giving you space?"

"Oh my God, Carla, please! I'm fucking just reading a book. I don't want to talk. Ain't nothing wrong with

me, but I should be asking you if anything's wrong."
Serenity stood up and walked to the china cabinet. She
stretched to the top of it and picked up an envelope and
threw it at Carla. "When were you going to tell me that
we might be losing the house? I didn't know you took
out a second mortgage."

"Oh, that's old. Look at the date. It was like a month
ago. Everything is good now. Who the fuck you think
you barking at anyway?" Carla shouted back.

Serenity scanned the paper for the date. *It is a month
ago!* Her face flushed with embarrassment. "Sorry,"
Serenity said in a low, defeated voice.

"We ain't losing Momma house," Carla stated loudly,
then continued in a calmer tone, "Where the fuck you
been anyway? I don't see you around here anymore."

Serenity walked back over to the sofa and took a seat
before she spoke. "Carla, you know my schedule. Between classes and that job I am booked solid!"

"That ain't all that's filling your time. What, think
I don't know that you been seeing Cass almost every
night?" Carla asked, beginning to laugh.

Serenity smiled, but it was faint. "So what? You been
keepin' tabs on me? You got someone following me,
watching my every move?" Serenity's tone became defensive and combative. "Can you tell me if I drank enough
fuckin' water yesterday, 'cause I can't remember?" Serenity snapped and stood to her feet.

"Serenity, you can't be fuckin' serious. What, you got
some dick and feel you could disrespect me like that? I
might not be yo' momma, but sure as hell, you goin' to
respect me." Carla stood in front of Serenity with her
arms folded on her chest. "Shit, 'cause of you I had to
take out a second mortgage. What you think, your lawyer and 'em trips I was takin' was fuckin' free? I didn't
allow them to give you a lawyer. I *paid* for one."

"So, I see," Serenity let out a loud sigh. "I almost got fucking killed by some crazy bitch, not you. You weren't fucking there! So, is it safe to say you blame me for Rock's death too . . .? Fuck you, Carla, I'm out," Serenity shouted, then stormed out of the house.

Carla rushed to the door and called out to Serenity, but she didn't turn around. She ran straight to her car and peeled out. "Fuck!" Carla screamed and slammed the front door shut. It felt like she had been down this road once before. She couldn't figure out if this attitude was about her and Cass, or something else.

Rico stood behind the bar smiling because today, he would get paid after revealing some info. Every Monday afternoon, he and Heaven would go to each bar in the restaurant/lounge and take inventory. Since that night when those rappers came in, she had been avoiding him. He figured she knew that he knew about her little secret. And that was why she was avoiding him.

Heaven walked to the bar to see Rico smiling. She knew what his grin was all about. *I hope this ain't gonna be some question-and-answer shit! I got to focus and get this shit done in a hurry,* she thought.

"Hey, there, Miss Heaven, happy to see you," Rico said.

"Boy, you know I'm busy. How else is this place gonna run?" Heaven replied, thinking if she didn't bring up nothing he would get the hint.

"I know that right, girl. So, never got to see you after that superstardom night." Rico pretended to be excited over Eminem's appearance at the restaurant.

"Right. I was running around here making sure security was on point. It was a madhouse in here. Don't you remember?" Heaven wished she hadn't asked that question.

"Yes, I do." Rico eyed Heaven as if to say, "Just tell me."

"What? Why you actin' like that? Listen, we got work to do, so I think we better start it," Heaven said sternly, almost demanding.

"You know what? I ain't gonna bullshit you no more. Look, I like you, but I ain't your friend, so don't take it any way. Listen, I'm gonna make you my offer . . ."

Heaven stepped back and put her hand on her hip. She convinced herself that denial was always the best role in situations like this. "Rico, what are you fuckin' talkin' 'bout? Offer? What offer? If you don't stop your shit right now and help me get this work done, your ass is fired," Heaven said, hoping her threat was clear.

"Oh, hell, no!" Rico shouted, causing some eyes to turn. He quickly flashed a smile to hide the fact that everything was not okay. "That's why I don't like your ass. But I'ma give you my price anyway . . . Six thousand every month, I can take my vacation anytime I like, and I also get a promotion." Rico stared at Heaven, giving her the impression that he wasn't backing down.

"Rico, why the fuck would I do that for you? You can pack yo'—"

Rico moved closer to Heaven and whispered in her ear, "'Cause you lickin' a certain sweet clit that your brother ain't even get to taste yet."

Heaven could feel her skin turning red all over, especially her face. A single thought rushed her head, *My brother can't find out.*

"Yeah, uh-huh. I thought you'd understand. What? You think my ears ain't open around here? I know Cass ain't hit that yet, but it seems you have." Rico continued in a low tone assuring no one could hear. "You see, your brother, he too much for his damn self. Since he been with Serenity, do you know how many times he has sat at this very bar goin' on about her? Most of the time he had just dropped her home and she still ain't even let him feel the pussy. He would say all type of shit when he was drunk." Rico looked at Heaven, wondering if he should keep going.

"Rico . . . um . . ." Heaven was in shock. She knew Cass wasn't sleeping with Serenity because he was sleeping with everyone else on the low. When she and Serenity would go shopping and hanging out, Cass would be out with other females.

The bar phone rang. No one reached for it. Rico stared at Heaven, and she kept her eyes on the floor. The ringing stopped. Another two minutes went by, and the phone began to ring again. This time it snapped Heaven from her bout of shame and humiliation.

"All Things Good, how can I help you?" Heaven answered the phone speaking slowly, trying to cover her shaky voice.

"Hello? Is th . . ." a female voice said trying to finish her sentence before the phone went dead.

Heaven hung up the phone, not waiting for the woman to finish. She heard enough to know who it was. She turned to Rico and said, "Come to my office before you leave for the night."

She walked swiftly, trying not to look anyone in their faces. Tears flooded her eyes. Her embarrassment made her feel ashamed. Her world felt closed with a cloud of shame hovering over her. She reached her office and closed the door behind her. Her knees buckled, and she slid down against the door to the floor, sobbing. "My brother would disown me," she said out loud, then continued, "How could Rico do this to me?" *'Cause my brother been runnin' his fucking mouth,* she answered her question in thought.

Heaven got up from the floor, grabbed some tissues from her desk, and wiped her eyes dry. She tossed the tissue in the garbage and took a seat behind her desk. All of a sudden, her world became darker. She remembered the woman she hung up the phone on. She dropped her head into the palm of her left hand resting on top of the desk.

Questions with no answers ran through her head. *How did she get the bar number? Who gave it to her? Is Rico and her in on this together? Is my brother fucking with her? That chick said she ain't have a phone, only a computer, lying cunt! How could I be so dumb? I should'a known better than to fuck with some random chick I met at a fuckin' game. I thought it was good because no one knew about her and she could be my escape.*

Heaven's thoughts consumed her. When she met Tootsie at the game, she was attracted and knew why she engaged her in a friendly conversation. A few days later, she contacted Heaven through Facebook and since then, they talked via the Web all the time. Their sexual desires developed almost instantaneously through e-mails, live messaging, and Skype. Her memories of watching Tootsie play with her pussy and getting fucked by some dude flooded her. Heaven loved the fact that Tootsie wasn't in a rush to meet because she felt the same way. She wanted to believe if Tootsie was kept at arm's length her brother wouldn't find out about it and she could eventually move away and live the life she wanted to.

She opened her desk drawer, pulled out a small bottle of Ketel One, and opened it immediately. The liquid moved slowly down her throat and a warm feeling hit her chest. She sat there not knowing for the first time her next move. There's one thing her brother always told her. He said he didn't care about other people and their sexual preferences, but he wouldn't have none of that shit in his family. *I should'a known that my cover would be blown one day,* she thought as she took another swig of the bottle. *I have to tell Serenity . . .*

Serenity parked her car in the lot of Cass's restaurant and dialed his number hoping he was there.

"Serenity, what's up? I didn't expect to—"

"Cass, tell me you're at the restaurant," Serenity's sniffles became louder.

"Baby, what's wrong? Where are you?" Cass spoke into the phone concerned.

"I'm . . . parked in the lot in back of the restaurant . . . Please, Cass, I need you . . ." Serenity begged.

"I'm walking out to you right now." Cass rushed through the back exit and saw Serenity in her car, crying.

He walked up to the driver's side and opened the door. He grabbed Serenity's hands and pulled her close to his chest, whispering, "Serenity, it's okay . . . it's okay. I got you, baby, . . . I got you . . . shhh . . . shhhh . . ."

Serenity stood there in his strong arms not wanting him to let go. She lifted her head and looked into his light eyes and said, "Can we go to your place?"

Cass was shocked. Since they'd been seeing each other, she'd never gone to his house. She either met him at the restaurant, or he would pick her up and go out somewhere. She played hard to get when it came to dropping those drawers, but she was the only female that caught his attention on a serious level. "If that's what you want to do, Serenity," he answered with a safe response. He tried to ease apart from her because his dick was getting hard at the thought of her in his house so close to his bed.

"Okay, let me go inside and tie up a few loose ends. You can tell the parking attendant to put your car in the garage and have my car ready, okay, baby?" Cass squeezed her hands and went back into the restaurant.

Serenity got her purse out and pulled out some tissue to wipe her eyes and nose. She took her keys out of the ignition and walked over to the attendant's booth outside. She explained to him what Cass said and waited for his return. Serenity wanted to feel loved not smothered, and with Cass's arms wrapped around her tightly, she didn't second-guess herself.

Cass stepped into the restaurant toward the main bar. "Yo, Rico, you and my sister good? I thought I saw some friction between y'all," he said.

"Not at all. Why? She told you different?" Rico asked, hoping his spot wasn't blown.

"She ain't tell me shit yet! I hope she don't have to either. Listen, I'ma be home for the rest of the evening, but I will be back before you lock up at two A.M. to do the count," Cass said, trusting him to call if things got crazy.

"No, problem," Rico said, wanting him to leave so he could find Heaven and work out the details of his safety net.

Cass turned around and headed toward the back exit. Thoughts were racing in his head. *What the fuck is wrong with her? She don't got no bruises or nothin'. Fuck, I hope she ain't one of these stalker bitches; play nice at first, then bust out the ropes. Shit, for all I know, her sex could be wackier than a mothafucker! Then, I'ma really have to leave her ass alone!*

Cass stood at the exit and, before opening the door, he said out loud, "Remember, act concerned. Wait for the opportunity. Then, swoop in." He walked out with confidence and quickly put a somber look on his face before entering his car.

Chapter 12

Iris jumped out of the cab and walked into the hotel lobby to see Carla waiting for her. She flashed a smile to play nice. "Sorry, Carla, I got a little tied up," Iris said, kissing her on the cheek. "Come on, let's go up to my room and handle our business. Is that okay with you?"

"Yeah, that's cool. Lead the way so I can enjoy the view," Carla spoke in a low voice.

"I'm sure you will," Iris mumbled as she walked like a supermodel hitting the runways.

"Don't shake it too hard. I don't want it to break," Carla said, as she trailed Iris to the elevator watching her phat rump rock from side to side.

Iris walked into the elevator slowly; she could feel Carla's eyes piercing her round asset.

Carla followed close behind, cornering her in the confined space. "What floor?"

"Three, please," Iris said, staring at Carla, hoping she wouldn't make a move on her now. She wanted to have the power. If Iris controlled the environment, she could definitely predict the outcome.

The elevator chimed in a mechanical voice, "Third floor. Please watch your step." The doors opened.

Iris noticed Carla wasn't moving to let her off the elevator. "Carla, are we going to get out or shall we stay in this cramped-ass space so you can stare at me all night?"

Carla held out her hand to stop the elevator doors from closing. Iris quickly shuffled out and started to walk to her room door.

Arriving, she reached into her purse and pulled out her key card to open the door. She turned the doorknob to enter once the green light flashed.

Carla didn't know what was about to go down, but she liked the signs Iris was giving.

"Have a seat. You want me to call room service for anything?" Iris showed Carla to the sofa and walked toward the bedroom.

Carla took a seat on the sofa and answered, "Nah, I'm good."

Iris came back walking toward Carla with a white envelope. She sat across from Carla and handed it to her.

"Thanks," Carla offered, then placed the envelope on the small table beside her.

"So, Carla, tell me, do you like what you see?" Iris opened her legs, slightly exposing her hairless pussy.

"I think you already know the answer to that question. Besides, why, all of a sudden, you now tryin' to get my mouth wet?" Carla questioned, suspicious of her sudden come-on.

Iris closed her legs. "Okay, I guess a little bit of fun won't be in our cards tonight," she said, sounding disappointed.

"I think we better get business out of the way first, then, maybe, we could have a bit of fun," Carla said.

"I thought we already took care of business. Didn't you get your money?" Iris asked, rising to her feet. She walked over to the small minibar and pulled out two bottles of vodka.

"Yeah . . . but . . ." Carla stuttered her words.

"But what?" Iris handed a glass and a bottle of vodka to Carla.

"I'm a little curious about you. I really can't figure you out. I know you get money and a lot of big playas affiliate themselves with you," Carla said, emptying the liquid into her glass.

"Oh, I think you're far from curious. Seems to me that you know exactly what you want," Iris giggled, pouring vodka into her glass.

"You got jokes. Ha-ha. I've been dealing with you for the past month, and I still can't figure why you helping *me* out. You don't know me. The only time I saw you was at Rock's funeral, and we didn't even talk for that long. Now, after a year, I call you out of the blue, and you willing to put paper in my pockets without even knowing me. That's a little suspect," Carla explained.

"I better hit the minibar again. Want some more?" Iris offered, contemplating if she should tell Carla the truth.

"Nah, I'm good."

"Carla, I know that you found out about me and Rock. And when I showed my face at the funeral, it was obvious you didn't tell Serenity. I guess my way of thanking you was helping you out whenever you needed me. That's why I gave you my number at the funeral. I'm happy you held on to it. Tell me, why didn't you tell her?" Iris's voice became softer, almost a whisper.

Carla stood up and sat next to Iris on the opposite sofa. "That ain't my business to tell her if she never suspected. He never treated her wrong, so who am I to deny love it's freedom. You know what I mean, sweetheart?" Carla's eyes roamed to Iris's sharp cleavage.

Iris took Carla's fingers and guided them over the nipple of her breast. Carla immediately parted Iris's legs with her free hand and rubbed her fingers gently over her clit. She could feel the wetness beginning to form under her fingertips as she moved them in a circular motion.

The moans from Iris's lips made Carla think twice about how fast she was able to uncover her most prized possession. Carla didn't want to abruptly stop Iris's pleasure. She continued to massage Iris's clit without voicing any emotions.

Iris continued to moan, enjoying her fun without noticing Carla's lack of passion. She reached her climax swiftly.

Carla removed her fingers and put them in Iris's mouth. She sucked the juices off with her. Then Carla looked at the side table beside the sofa opposite them. She picked up the envelope and headed for the door.

"So, that's it? Is that all you gonna allow me to feel?" Iris asked, disappointed.

Carla turned around and said, "*You* said a little fun. I think I met the requirement." She smiled, then added, "Besides, I got some work to do. Didn't you say you needed two more girls?" Carla reminded her.

"Absolutely correct, but that shouldn't interrupt our fun . . ." Iris was annoyed.

"I'm sure you know how to have lots of fun. I doubt you need me around. I'll call you when I get the girls." Carla opened the entrance door so Iris couldn't lure her back to her pussy.

"Now, you're funny. We *will* talk," Iris said with a smile.

"Yeah, I'ma see ya." Carla shut the door behind her, happy to leave. She needed to focus on why Iris showed a side of her that she never indicated before. *I'm just gettin' started if she really tryin' to take this route. She could have anyone though. Why she tryin' to play that role with me since I only been dealin' wit' her for a short time?* she questioned, riding the elevator down.

Iris did not mind the momentary company. As long as she controlled the situation she was happy. She got her pussy rubbed to climax, and that was good enough. Iris already knew Serenity's schedule, so there was no reason to take Carla beyond a little fun. Iris was pleased with herself. She prepared for a shower and bed. Tomorrow, she had an early flight back to D.C.

"Don't tease me, baby. Fuck this pussy . . . harder, you fucking . . . harder, Stuckey, harder . . . Oh yeah, that's it! Show me, mothafucker . . . You cumming baby?" Tootsie screamed, then put her face into the pillow. She rocked her ass back and forth, gliding on his rock-hard wood.

Stuckey's face began to shift and his strokes became tougher and faster. His shaft was throbbing, and the pressure was building. "Here it comes, baby . . . Come put it in your mouth . . . Ahhh, shit, damn that pussy's good," Stuckey said as he slapped his still-hard cock against her lips.

Tootsie sucked the tip of his dick until she emptied every last drop of cum into her mouth. Then Stuckey headed to the bathroom to take a shower. Tootsie followed.

"Hey, baby, when do you think I'ma blow this coop?" Tootsie sat on the toilet to relieve her bladder as Stuckey stepped under the steamy, running water.

"Tootsie, you remember why we here?" Stuckey lathered up his washcloth with soap.

"Because . . . I want it over with and . . . I was thinking that maybe me and you . . . can be together . . ." Tootsie said in a soft voice, joining Stuckey under the water. She stood close to him, allowing her naked body to press against his.

Stuckey dropped his washrag and wrapped his arms around her body. He placed his hands on each ass cheek and pulled her naked body closer. His tongue found her nipples. His dick was rising. Tootsie lifted her leg so his wood could slip into her pink hole. Stuckey squeezed her ass tighter as he entered her flesh. He leaned her against the tiled wall of the shower. His strokes were passionate; slow and deep. Their moans grew louder and louder as they both continued to fulfill each other's climaxes.

Stuckey didn't want to talk about the future with Tootsie. He already knew her future. Instead, he used his dick to do the talking for him. He loved having a steady woman next to him. He never had any girl-friends. There were only three rules to go by: talk to the pussy, fuck the pussy, then move on to the next pussy. He was fighting his feelings of falling for Tootsie. He didn't want to, but he's never been cooped up with one woman for so long. The last time he was with a woman this long it was his mother.

Tootsie took care of him while she was on lockdown in the hotel room for what seemed like forever. She made sure Stuckey's every sexual need was fulfilled. If he wanted to fuck, suck, slap, she was willing and able. When he talked, she listened and never voiced an opinion. Of course, he could come and go as he wanted. But the most she could do was walk out onto the balcony for fresh air. Tootsie took all the opportunities she could to seduce and pussy-whip Stuckey. Her efforts didn't disappoint her when she noticed him staying in the hotel more than usual now.

Chapter 13

Cass opened the driver-side door to his car. Serenity was already in the passenger's seat. Her eyes were still damp from crying. He wanted to ask her what was wrong but figured she would let him know in her own time. He just wanted to get her to his house as fast as possible so she didn't change her mind.

Silence filled the car on the way to his house. Serenity stared out of the window watching the trees blow in the wind. Cass placed his hand on her thigh. She remembered when Rock used to do that. She missed that touch. Serenity wanted someone near her, someone that could show her the love she was looking for. It was time. She was ready.

Cass pulled into his garage attached to his two-story house. He pressed a button to close the garage door as he parked. Then he turned to Serenity and said, "This is where I live."

"Well, this is a nice garage," Serenity said, laughing. "Who lives in the house?" She continued to laugh getting out of the car.

"Funny. You know what I mean. Come on, follow me." Cass led her through a door leading into his house.

Serenity entered a short hallway that opened out into a spacious room that looked like a game room. There stood a pool table and two forty-five inch plasma TVs covering the wall with game systems set on the table in front of them. There was a stuffed marlin fish on a plaque on the opposite wall. Huge leather recliners were spaced perfectly throughout the grand room. It had the bachelor feel and definitely the look.

She continued to follow him. He led her through a kitchen with marble countertops and shining stainless steel appliances. Serenity entered his living area; it was big enough to fit her bedroom ten times over. She took a seat on a plush white leather sofa and placed her bag on the coffee table.

Cass walked past her, took his blazer off, and threw it to the opposite sofa. He stopped and pushed the wall with his finger. To her surprise, the wall opened, exposing some stereo equipment. Hits from Maxwell swirled softly through the ceiling.

He walked toward Serenity. "You want something to drink, eat, anything?" Cass asked.

"Maybe some water would be good. This is a nice place. I wonder what the upstairs looks like," Serenity hinted at her intentions.

Cass was already headed for the kitchen when her words stopped him in his tracks. He said nothing until he came back with her water and sat down next to her. "Umm, Serenity, are you sure? I mean, I don't want you to feel pressured or anything like that," Cass spoke in a soft tone.

"Cass"—she took the bottle of water out of his hand and straddled him—"I want you inside me. What you waitin' on?" She allowed her whispers to lightly tickle his ear.

Serenity didn't have to say another word.

Cass picked her up in his strong arms and carried her up to his bedroom. He laid her down on his white cotton, fifteen-hundred thread count Egyptian sheets. Slowly, he started to remove her clothing. He felt her soft skin and sucked on her ripe nipples. She moaned slightly. He moved his lips and tongue to her hot spot. Cass worked his oral game like clockwork, and it only took five minutes before Serenity's legs were trembling and his mouth was filled with cum. He took his cue and removed his pants and underwear. His eleven-inch cock stood at attention. He looked down at Serenity's shaved pussy glistening with wetness. He opened her legs and gently entered her hot box. His entire shaft was immediately wrapped with the warmth of her throbbing flesh. Their lovemaking lasted for a couple of hours.

Cass lay there looking up at the ceiling. Serenity was sound asleep. He glanced at the time. It was almost one-thirty in the morning. He eased out of the bed and headed to his master bathroom for a quick shower. Cass was certain Serenity wasn't going to wake up any time soon after the session he just put her through. He decided after his shower he would head out to All Things Good and check out the bus depots for any easy victims.

He examined himself in the full-length mirror in his walk-in closet. Then he entered back into his bedroom and looked at Serenity. She was beautiful, and now that she finally gave herself to him, he was willing to see where she would fit into his life. He looked through his pants pockets on the floor and recovered his wallet. Then silently, he eased out of the room and headed for the garage.

Cass got into his car and drove to the restaurant. Thirty minutes later, he pulled into his reserved parking spot on the lot and saw people lingering outside deciding on who and what they were doing next. He turned the ignition off, got out of the car, and entered the restaurant through the back exit. Rico stood at the bar cleaning up.

"Hey, looks like we had a good night," Cass stated.

"Um . . . Yeah, we cleared five thousand at this bar alone. I'm waiting for the tallies at the other two bars in the lounge area," Rico said tired.

"A'ight . . . Heaven still here?" Cass asked.

"Yeah, she's in her office. When I have all the money together, I'll bring it to her office for you," Rico said.

"Cool," Cass replied. He left the bar and went to Heaven's office. His face was beaming when he knocked on her door, then entered. "What up . . .?"

"Hey, Cass, what you all happy about?" Heaven questioned.

"Oh, I think my lifestyle just changed," he replied.

"What the hell is that supposed to mean? What, you hit the fuckin' lottery?" Heaven joked.

"Ah, somethin' like that. Serenity is back at my house, butt-ass naked in my bed," he exclaimed.

"So, you finally got some. What does that mean?" she tried to sound as if his words didn't sting.

"It feels different. Like she's the type of female who can satisfy my needs—" Cass was interrupted.

"Your needs? What, so you sayin' I don't have to cover for yo' ass no more? Like she gonna be yo' only chick you with now?" Heaven became annoyed.

"Yeah, basically. Why you got an attitude? You mad?" Cass asked surprised.

"Mad? Why would I be mad? I don't give a fuck where you stick your dick!"

"Damn, I thought you would be happy that I actually want to settle down," he said.

"Well, that's good, then maybe yo' ass can be around here and actually do some work," Heaven voiced.

"Damn, why the fuck you bitchin'? I'ma go so you don't spoil my mood. Rico gonna bring all the money from the bar into your office for me. Put it in the safe and

I'll make the deposit later," Cass stated, then walked out the door.

He left the restaurant a little upset but wouldn't let Heaven's bitchy attitude ruin his disposition. Cass wanted to head back to his house but had to check out some prospects before going back. He walked out of the back exit and went to his car.

After hopping into his black, dark tinted BMW 6 Series, he cruised the streets. Detroit was ghetto as hell. Liquor stores, churches, and hair salons sat on every corner, but as Cass entered the city's main bus depot he smiled. He was from the D through and through. Now that his money was overflowing, and he finally had someone to share it with, a great sense of security centered in him. He pulled into the bus depot's lot, parked his car, and headed inside to get a bottle of water and to scan the young women waiting around for their pickups.

He noticed a young girl who couldn't have been more than nineteen years old. She stood leaning against a pay phone showing her tight, black True Religion jeans and a white tank top. Her hair was straight and rested on her shoulders. From the stance, he knew she was having a tough time. He walked closer to her while looking around for any hungry eyes. Cass pretended he needed to use the pay phone next to her.

"Excuse me, but you wouldn't happen to have any change, would you?" Cass flashed a friendly smile.

The young female turned around and looked up and down. "What's the matter with the phone on your hip?" She quickly let him know she wasn't about any games.

Cass looked at his hip. He was busted and had to come up with something quick. "Phone dead," he said.

"I guess I ain't the only one around here with a dead phone. But, nah, I don't got no more change. I just used my last tryin' to get my cousin on the phone," she said with a sigh.

"What, you need a ride?" Cass asked, a little too eager.

She looked at his face and screwed hers up. "You think I'm stupid, huh? Look, you think you the only pimp to approach me? Please!"

Cass laughed and stood back with his hands in the air. "First of all, chick, I ain't a pimp. Second, I have legit money. Third, you ain't too smart," he said brazenly.

"Ain't too smart? Nigga, you better get the fuck outta my face," her voice got louder.

"It seems to me that any smart person would have their ride already waiting on them. Especially if you know about some of these unsavory characters that hang around here." His voice lowered. "Anyway, thanks, and sorry I ever bothered you. You have a good night"— he looked at his watch—"I mean, a good morning." He started to walk away.

The young girl thought about it and didn't really want to stand around the bus depot attracting unwanted attention. There was a diner across the street. Maybe she could go there and vibe him out. After all, she did need a ride. "You could join me for somethin' to eat across the street. If not, then you can get some change there."

Cass looked at her. "Well, I could use some breakfast, I guess . . . Why not?" He walked beside her out of the bus station toward the diner.

"Umm . . . My name is Cass, by the way. We better hurry. It looks like it just started to rain," he said.

They both rushed across the street to get out of the rain. The smell of bacon and hash browns hit them as soon as the door opened. They found a booth to sit in and waited for the waitress to offer them some menus.

"So, you didn't tell me your name," Cass mentioned.

"It's Carmen," she replied, sticking her hand out to shake his.

The waitress came to their booth and handed them the menus. She waited for them to place their order. When she finished scribbling on her pad, she took the menus and headed back to the kitchen.

Carmen sat a little on edge. She didn't know who this guy was. She sure as hell didn't want him to think she was one of those girls looking for a "daddy."

"So, where you from?" Cass finally asked.

"Maryland. I came here to visit my cousin," she answered.

"That's cool. I know a few cats from the Baltimore area. So, what's up with yo' cousin? She ain't answering her phone?" Cass asked.

"Yeah, she like that sometimes," Carmen said as she watched the waitress walk toward the table with their food. She placed the bill turned over on the table after she served the platters.

"Oh," he replied as he broke the runny egg with his fork.

"I know the address, but obviously, she done forgot that she had to pick me up," Carmen said between bites of fluffy buttermilk pancakes.

"That's fucked up," Cass grinned.

"Well, I don't find it funny. I'ma knock that bitch silly when I see her," Carmen said with a mouthful. "Why were you at the station? Were you supposed to pick somebody up?"

"Nah, I dropped my boy off, but I was thirsty as hell so I came in to buy a bottle of water. Then, that's when I saw you." Cass continued, "I was about to call my sister but noticed my phone was dead."

"So what do you do, Cass, if you don't mind me asking?" Carmen sounded interested.

"I work with food," he answered, not wanting to give her any details.

"So, you a fry cook then, huh?" Carmen joked.

"Far from that, baby girl, far from that," he said feeling a bit insulted. He took a final bite of his toast and thoughts ran through his head. *This is too much fuckin' work. I could be fuckin' home right now sticking my dick into some sweet pussy. I better go the bathroom and call Serenity before she wakes up and don't find me around.*

Cass rose to his feet. "Excuse me, I'll be right back."

"Nigga, you ain't stickin' me with this bill, so you better put your half on the table," Carmen said firmly.

"Wow, I hear that," Cass said as he reached into his pocket and pulled out a fifty-dollar bill and placed it on the table. He walked toward the bathroom.

I definitely don't need this shit, he thought as he quickly stepped into the bathroom. He pulled out his phone and dialed her number. It rang but went straight to voice mail. He tried again, but he still got Serenity's voice mail. He dialed his house number and a groggy voice answered on the other end.

"Hey . . . Cass, where . . . Where are you?" Serenity turned to lie on her side with the phone close to her ear.

"I had to close the restaurant, baby. I just wanted to make sure you good. You can go back to sleep. I'll be back in a little while," he assured her.

"That's sweet," she said ready to close her eyes.

"See you in a minute," Cass said before hanging up the phone. He left the bathroom and walked back to the booth.

Carmen placed his change in front of him as he sat down. "Thanks, but you could've just paid for everything with the money I left."

"Nah, no need for a handout," Carmen lied. She had ten dollars left, and that wasn't going to be enough to get her where she needed to go.

"A'ight, Carmen, it was nice to meet you. I hope you get to your cousin's house safely," Cass said preparing to leave the booth.

"Um, Cass . . . um . . . You think you can give me a ride over there? I just wanna jump into a shower and get some sleep," she said in her sweetest voice.

"I don't usually do this . . . but you seem like a nice girl. You said you have the address? Let me see," he requested.

Carmen reached into her pocket, pulled out a piece of paper, and handed it to him.

Cass looked at the address, then looked at her. "This is in the opposite direction of where I'm going, but I can . . . I mean, I would like to put you in a cab. It would make me feel better knowing that you weren't just sitting around this place," he smiled.

"Well, if you insist. Thank you," Carmen flashed her pearly whites.

The two of them walked out of the diner and headed to the cab stand. He helped Carmen get into the vehicle.

She turned to him and said, "I hope you're being nice because you are. And not—"

"If I wasn't, I wouldn't have cared. Write down my number so you can call me just to let me know you're safe. Is that okay?" Cass asked.

"Yeah, okay. Listen, thanks, and I'm sorry if I came off a little defensive. I'm just not used to . . . nice people," she added reaching for a pen out of her pocketbook.

Cass recited his number to her, then closed the cab door. He watched the cab pull off. He glanced at his watch again. It was approaching four and his eyes were heavy. He strolled back to his car in the lot, pulled out his keys, and pressed the unlock button. After he got in, he started the ignition. He drove out of the bus depot proud of his latest prospect. Carmen didn't know it yet, but her life was going to change. *Young, dumb, and full of cum,* his thoughts made him laugh out loud.

Chapter 14

Serenity put the phone back onto its base and lay back, pulling the sheets over her chest. Her eyes were closed, and she was thinking of the passion she was just a part of. *Well, he definitely can hold his own!* A smile formed on her lips. Quickly, she jumped up and ran downstairs. Serenity reached for her purse and pulled out her phone. She looked around feeling a light chill, so she walked her naked body back to Cass's bedroom with her phone in hand. She got back under the covers on the bed. Serenity looked at her phone and saw Cass called her a couple of times. The next missed-call number she saw made her reality set in on what she had done—Heaven called.

"Oh my God, what have I done? I just fucked her brother," she said out loud. "But I don't want to give up what I have with her." *Besides, she ain't gonna say shit 'cause she don't want her brother to know she feelin' girls,* her thoughts swirled. She admitted and accepted her feelings for women. She loved the touch of soft light hands caressing her body, but there were times where she wanted a strong grip to hold her. When she came to Detroit, she didn't think of ever meeting another female, let alone touching one.

Since she'd been seeing Cass, her relationship with Heaven increased. She always saw her when she came to the restaurant, and Cass encouraged their growing friendship. It began as just conversations on the phone but soon grew to much more than that. Then, Heaven began to invite her out to parties and plan spa days, courtesy of Cass. She remembered the first time they went to the spa.

"Girl, you crazy! I think you done had too much champagne . . ." Serenity laughed.

"What? Don't you think you should get what you paid for? Shit, as much as I come here, they should know better," Heaven said between sips from her glass.

"But, Heaven, it wasn't like you couldn't have the massage. It just wouldn't be the person you want. It wouldn't of killed you to compromise," she said.

"Well, I can't be relaxed when heavy, rough hands are rubbing me all over." Heaven didn't realize what she said.

"Yeah, I guess you right." Serenity looked at her face, then continued, "But sometimes those heavy hands can be just what you need." Her eyes met with Heaven's. Heaven was gorgeous; her skin was flawless, and her body was to die for. Serenity couldn't remember seeing a woman who even came close to her type of beauty. She felt starstruck for a moment, but was just as impressed when Heaven seemed equally intrigued.

"Not for me. I like a soft touch," Heaven took her fingers and gently moved them up and down the middle of Serenity's back.

A door opening shook Serenity out of her trip down memory lane. *I'm gonna have to tell her,* she admitted in her head. She set the phone on the night table and quickly pretended she was asleep. She could hear his footsteps as he entered. Five minutes later she felt his warm skin spoon her body. She drifted off to sleep.

Serenity woke up to sunlight hitting her eyes. She didn't feel Cass's body next to her. She turned to find him sprawled out beside her, snoring loudly. She moved off the bed slowly, reducing the chances of him waking up. She grabbed her phone, then her clothes off the floor, and quietly headed into the bathroom.

Serenity wanted to get dressed and leave. She wanted to talk to Heaven. She felt she had to explain. She walked out of the bathroom fully clothed and could still hear Cass's loud snores. She decided on not waking him and left the bedroom. As she headed downstairs for her shoes, she dialed a cab number and requested a driver. She put her shoes on and left through the front door. While she waited for the cab outside she called Heaven.

"Hey," Heaven answered.

"You at the restaurant yet? I gotta talk to you," Serenity said trying not to beg.

"Yeah, I'm here alone. Come on, 'cause Rico and the rest of the staff will be here in an hour. Bye." Heaven hung up the phone, annoyed.

I wonder if she gonna tell me about her and Cass. I know it ain't none of my business 'cause she don't want to fuck up her wants either, Heaven thought sitting at her desk. She had the face of a jealous lover and didn't like it. A short time later she was disturbed by the ringing of her phone.

"Can you let me in? I'm at the back exit close to your office." Serenity listened for an answer.

"Yeah, I'm coming." Heaven hung up the phone and proceeded to go let Serenity in.

Serenity's face had the look of shame on it. She walked past Heaven once she opened the door and walked into her office.

Heaven followed behind her watching her ass in her tight, stonewashed jeans. She said nothing until she sat behind her desk. "So, what brings you by so early?"

"Um, I . . . I need to tell you something."

"Can you stop delaying and just tell me. You know I don't like to play games," Heaven quickly reminded her.

"I slept with Cass last night." Serenity waited for a response.

"So, what does that have to do with me? I'm not Cass's wife. I'm his sister. Why should that bother me?" Heaven asked the question, hiding the green in her eyes.

"I know but"—Serenity got closer to Heaven—"I . . . I don't want to stop what we just began."

"Well, I think . . . We don't have to stop," Heaven said, surprising herself with her words.

Serenity was thrown aback by Heaven's selfish words. She paused and admitted that having her cake with ice cream wouldn't be so bad. "So—"

Heaven put her fingers on Serenity's lips to stop her from talking. She kissed her passionately. Their tongues intertwined like two slippery snakes searching for prey. Heaven rubbed her pussy through her jeans.

Serenity let out a soft moan.

Heaven continued to play with her tongue and slid her free hand under Serenity's shirt. Her fingers eased Serenity's bra up to expose her firm nipples. Serenity felt Heaven's fingers pinching her nipple lightly, not causing any pain. Serenity's clit became hard, and her nipples were stiff. They continued to tantalize each other, not paying any mind to their soundings.

It was almost eight when Rico unlocked the back door to begin his long day's work. He opened the door and started to walk down the hallway. Then he thought his hearing was playing tricks with him, so he stopped and stood still. He could hear someone moaning. He quietly crept down the short hallway and stopped in front of Heaven's office.

The moaning didn't stop. It was obvious where it was coming from. He turned around and headed back to the exit. Rico didn't want Cass to walk in on them. *Shit, I can't have him fuckin' up my easy money,* he thought as he turned around quietly. He reached the exit and opened the door, then slammed it shut. He started singing loudly and even did a little two-step by the door. He entered, making sure his noise could be heard behind closed doors.

Heaven abruptly stopped, hearing the loud soprano-like voice entering through the back door. She motioned to Serenity to be still and not say a word. Heaven waited. She could hear Rico's voice trailing into the main dining area.

"Serenity—"

"I'm leavin'. I'll sneak out the back," Serenity interrupted with a whisper.

Heaven watched as Serenity got dressed and snuck out of the office to the back entrance. *What is it about that chick? Her touch is so addictive. There's no way I want to stop this. I guess Cass may have some competition without even knowin' it.* Her thoughts flooded her mind.

Cass was awakened by his iPhone ringing. "Hello," he answered with a groggy, deep voice.

Shawn P sat on the balcony of his hotel room. He contemplated how he would talk to Cass. *I'ma just tell him a story. He don't know all of it ain't true. 'Cause I know one thing for sure; all this back and forth is putting a dent in my pocket. I can't delay this shit no more. It's time to spin the wheels.*

"Yo, Cass, what up?"

"Yo, what up, my dude? Everything good? You usually don't call a nigga this fuckin' early," Cass answered.

"You got time today? I need to holla at you for a minute. Can you swing by my hotel?" Shawn P put concern in his voice.

"A'ight, no doubt. I'ma be on my way in about twenty." Cass hung up the phone, apprehensive about their meeting.

He walked into his closet, only to be interrupted by another call. He looked at the caller ID and grinned. "Hey, baby, why you left like that?"

"I didn't mean to, but my sister needed the car early this morning," she lied. "I could come back later," she suggested.

Cass didn't want her to be too comfortable so he declined the offer. "Actually, it's a big day today. I got another celebrity dinner party to get ready for. I need a shape-up, and I gotta go pick up my suit from the cleaners, and I got meeting in twenty . . ." he said.

"Oh, I see. You get the cookie, then don't wanna stick around for the fortune," she joked.

"What? You must be smokin' fuckin' crack. Who wouldn't want you around them?"

"I'm only joking. Damn, almost sounds like you defensive about somethin'. Are you?" she asked a little puzzled.

"Nope, not at all," he said reassuring her.

"All right, well, get back to doin' whatever you was doin'. I'll talk to you later, baby." She hung the phone up.

Cass touched the word END on the screen of his phone.

***

"Yo, man, what's good?" Shawn P said holding out his hand to greet Cass. "Come in. You want somethin' to drink?"

"Nah, man, I'm good. Just a bit anxious on what you hollerin' 'bout." Cass got right down to business.

"I hear you. Well, I ain't no bitch. . . ." Shawn P started. "And, what I mean by that is I ain't one to believe all the chatter in the air. But I thought you should be told about what a little bird told me. Um, you been checkin' some girl named Serenity, right?" Shawn asked, sipping from a water bottle.

"Yeah, don't tell me you fucked her?" Cass didn't want a reply.

"Nah, ain't nothin' like that, fam. I was at a stripper function the other night, and her name came up. When it did, my ears perked up 'cause I heard you mention her name before. Well, niggas got to talkin' and drinkin', and they said she involved with some murder out in D.C. But you and I both know to find a ride-or-die chick these days is hard. That intrigued me, so I asked a few questions. Come to find out, she set some niggas up and took they stash," Shawn explained. "Her payday turned out to be close to half a mil' out on the street."

"Word . . . Why you tellin' me this?" Cass questioned.

"'Cause, I look out for my fam. And, I know your ear ain't really to the ground no more in the drug game. I know you tryin' to go legit now, even though you still dabblin' in some other shit too."

"Yo, Shawn, how you know it's the same chick?" Cass asked, skeptical about the story.

"'Cause they described her to me. I saw her that night I came when Eminem showed up," Shawn said. "But listen, that ain't the only reason I wanted to talk to you." Shawn continued, "I wanted to see if you would be down with somethin' . . . She got a price on her head."

"A price on her head?" Cass asked not believing what he was hearing.

"Yeah, two hundred k."

"And what you want me—" Cass stood up.

"Cass, sit down. I have an offer for you." He waited for Cass to return to his seat. "You ain't pullin' no trigger. That ain't in you no more. But since you already close to her, it would be an easy setup and an easier payday."

"Oh, man, I see . . ." Cass leaned back and looked up at the ceiling. "Hold on, Shawn. You say it's the same chick, and she got a contract out on her. My question to you is, why you need me? You know where she at, and I'm sure you got soldiers on standby. I may not be in that game no more, but I got sense."

"That's why I wanted to offer you an opportunity. You a businessman. Think about it," Shawn said calmly.

"Easy money, huh?" Cass repeated.

"If you ain't tryin' to get a piece of that two hundred, then I suggest you don't get too close to her 'cause a nigga goin' have to get at her." Shawn stood up.

"How long do I have 'til before you put your soldiers on the job?" Cass asked.

"You got a couple of days." Shawn picked up a blunt off the coffee table and lit it.

"Yeah, a'ight. You'll hear from me," Cass said walking toward the door.

"A'ight." Shawn held out his hand to give him some dap, then opened the door.

Cass walked to the elevators and pushed the down button. His mind was consumed with thoughts. *This can't be the same chick. But why do I even care? If she could set up some next dude, what makes me think she ain't tryin' to set my ass up? At least, that nigga got some respect by askin' me. After all, he is in my city.* Cass got back into his car and headed home.

Chapter 15

Carmen's thought of having a happy reunion with her older cousin was a slim chance. When she decided on surprising her cousin in Detroit, she thought it would be all good. Upon her arrival, she was hit with the hard truth.

When she arrived at the house in the wee hours that morning and knocked on the front door, Lele didn't answer. Her boyfriend Devon opened the door instead.

"Who the fuck is you?" Devon spat out.

Carmen looked at the number on the house, then the paper with the address on it before answering. "Um, I'm Carmen, Lele's cousin. You must be her boyfriend. Is she here?"

"That bitch is gone, and she ain't comin' back," he said with an angry slur.

"Okay, well, I tried to call her before I came down here, but my calls kept going to voice mail. My phone went dead, so I don't know if she called me back or not. Do you know where she went?" Carmen's voice was shaky.

"I ain't her fuckin' keeper," Devon's voice was loud.

"Sorry, I don't—"

"You don't mean to be fuckin' botherin' me! Get the fuck off my porch!" Devon slammed the door in her face.

Carmen sucked her teeth. She didn't know her surroundings and was now stuck. Lele was the only person

she knew in Detroit. But she was nowhere to be found.
She couldn't understand why she hadn't picked up her
phone. Carmen's surprise visit was a total mistake. She
should have stayed her ass in Maryland.

It was clear that Devon wasn't going to help her. She
was stranded by her own selfish intentions; surprising
Lele was supposed to be her escape. Carmen stood on
the porch not knowing what to do. She looked at the
piece of paper in her hand and turned it over. *Cass.
He didn't seem like the type that could hurt a fly. I got
no other choice,* she thought. Carmen started walking,
hoping she could find somewhere to use the phone.

"I'm sorry, did I wake you," a young female voice spoke.

"Who is this?" an aggravated voice replied.

"Carmen. Remember, you told me to call you so you
could know I'm safe," she said with an attitude.

Cass quickly answered, "Right, so you good?" He
spoke in a low voice, almost whispering. He walked to
the bathroom and peeked in to find Serenity nowhere
in sight. He slowly walked out to the hallway with the
phone to his ear. After his meeting with Shawn P, he
came home and fell asleep, not knowing if Serenity had
returned.

"Can you hold on a minute?" He didn't wait for a
reply, but stood completely still and listened for any
sounds downstairs. There were none. He put the phone
back to his ear. "Yeah, so you good?"

"Yeah," Carmen said, trying to hide her disappointed
feeling since arriving in Detroit.

"Sounds like you having a blast," he said.

"Look, I just wanted to call you and let you know I
was safe. That's all, so I'll let you go," Carmen's voice
sounded more than annoyed by his sarcasm.

"I'm just kidding. Sounds like you need a friend.
Why don't we meet up?" Cass asked, hoping for a positive response.

"I don't know. My situation is a little bleak right now. I just walked damn near a mile to find this pay phone," she admitted.

"What you mean?" Cass asked, now concerned about his future prospect.

"Well, when I got to my cousin's house, come to find out her boyfriend kicked her ass out. And now, I have no a clue about where she's at," Carmen added.

"Damn, Carmen, sorry to hear that," Cass said. "So, where you at?"

"I'm at some bookstore called Urban Knowledge. The manager was nice enough to let me use the phone. Ummm, I don't mean to get you involved, but do you think you—"

"Say no more. I know where you at. I know the manager. She's real sweet. Tell her you're a friend of mine. She'll hook you up. You can stay there until I come to pick you up. Don't worry, everything will work out. We'll find your cousin," Cass promised.

"Cass, you just don't know how grateful I am. Trust me, once we find my cousin, I'm outta your hair," Carmen said, relieved.

"Listen, I know how shit can be. Besides, I was hoping you would call. Just sit tight and I'll be there in a while. See you soon." Cass hung up the phone.

He walked back into his bedroom and glanced at the time. It was after nine in the morning. He was tired and felt like he just went to sleep. He entered his master bath for a shower to shake the sleepiness away.

"Need a ride?" a familiar voice filled the bookstore.

Cass's eyes penetrated Carmen and instantly made her secure. She blushed from his eagerness to help her. He wore Burberry cargo shorts with Burberry canvas kicks and a white V-neck T-shirt that fit his defined chest well. On his left wrist was a Rolex and a diamond stud pierced his right ear. He was handsome, and any woman would play damsel in distress for his rescue. She had to admit his kind heart made him that much more attractive.

"I sure do!" She picked up her bag and thanked the manager, then headed out of the bookstore.

Cass slipped the manager a fifty-dollar bill and followed behind Carmen. They stepped out of the store and walked to his car.

"I was hoping to see you again. I didn't think you was gonna call me. I'm glad it was sooner than later," Cass smiled, opening the passenger-side door for her.

"Thank you." Carmen blushed. It felt like her high school days. When she got in, she saw the custom leather seats and the fully loaded dash. She couldn't help but think that she picked a winner.

Cass closed the door and went around to the driver's side, then got in. "Where you think she's at?"

"Who?" Carmen asked, contemplating on how she could stay in his presence.

"Ummm, your cousin . . ."

"Oh, I'm sorry. My mind is so crazy right now. I came down here to surprise her, and she ain't nowhere to be found. My phone is dead. My money is nearly damn gone. I don't know what my cousin is into. I don't know if she hurt, dead, all right . . . nothing!" Carmen tried to hold back her tears.

"Mama, you don't have to worry about anything right now . . ." Cass's voice trailed off, "'cause you look like a hot mess," he said, trying to make her laugh.

"What?" Carmen yelled, not expecting to hear that. She quickly flipped the visor down. He was right. Her eyes were red with black circles around them. She tried to smooth her hair back into a ponytail.

"I'm just kiddin'. Don't kill me; I can't help it," Cass said smiling at her.

Carmen let out a fake laugh. She didn't feel like laughing. Her fate was in her hands. She didn't want to go back to Maryland and couldn't go anywhere without making sure Lele was okay. She looked at Cass and said, "I don't know what to do!"

"Like I said, don't worry about it. It will all work out," he said reassuring her.

"Where are we going anyway?" Carmen asked, searching for some tissue in her bag.

"Oh, well, I was going to take you to a hotel—"

"I told you I don't have money like that. You might as well stop the car. Let me use your phone so I can try my cousin again," Carmen said.

Cass did what he was told and pulled the car over, then put it in park. He passed his phone to her and watched her face intensely.

Carmen dialed Lele's number. It went to voice mail. She tried again, still no answer. She passed the phone back to him and began to cry with her hands covering her face.

Cass took his opportunity. "Listen, let me call my sister and see what I can do," he lied.

Cass dialed Iris's number and spoke into the phone briefly.

Carmen looked at him, wiping the tears from her eyes.

"You're in luck. My sister said you could stay with her for a couple of days 'til you get a hold of your cousin or decide to go back to Maryland," he said, hoping she would say yes.

"Seriously? But she don't even know me. I ain't 'bout to just show up at nobody house just like that," Carmen remarked.

"Listen, it's cool. She ain't even there. You'll have the house to yourself. Here's the key," he said holding it up to her.

"But . . ."

"But nothing!" Cass blasted, slapping Carmen into the passenger-side window.

"Oh, what the he—" Carmen let out a scream.

Cass proceeded to slapped her continuously until her lips and nose were bleeding. He opened his glove compartment and pulled out a wad of napkins, then threw them at her. "Take those and wipe your nose. I don't want no blood in my car. I just got this shit detailed." His voice was hard and forceful.

"Cass, I thought . . ." Carmen stuttered.

"You thought fuckin' nothin'," Cass said, relieved by his aggression. "Carmen, it works like this"—he cleared his throat—"usually I would play this game of 'oh, how much I'm feelin' you' kinda thing, but I got some disturbin' news today. So, I don't want to play the game, nor do I have the time," Cass spoke chastising her.

Carmen moved her hand slowly to her side. Her upper body fell on to her lap covering her hand easing to her purse. She gripped a small box cutter. Then she rocked her body back and forth crying loudly. She slightly looked up at Cass and noticed he was about to drive back into traffic. She knew if she didn't do something fast, this would be the worst day of her young life.

She lunged at him. The car swerved into oncoming traffic. Luckily, he missed the vehicles. Cass pulled back and hit the brakes hard, jerking their bodies by the sudden movement. Carmen was discombobulated by the chain of events.

He smacked her hard across the face. His fingers gripped her neck tightly. "What the fuck you tryin' to do? Kill us both? You so fuckin' stupid. Now, give me that shit before I get even angrier and take my frustrations out on you some more."

Carmen gave him the box cutter and watched him throw it out the window. She stopped crying. She was now scared. She thought she was going to piss, shit, and vomit all at the same time. Pain came over her face and head. She closed her eyes and prayed for her life.

Cass drove close to an hour in silence, deep in his thought. He finally stopped in front of a rundown motel. A few months back when he purchased the house out in Gary, he was paying weekly rent at this place. It was isolated with not a soul in sight for miles. A perfect place for training a potential ho. He stepped out of the car, then locked it, making sure Carmen couldn't escape.

She didn't even move. She was too shaken up.

He knocked on the door, and a female answered. He spoke a few words, then walked over to the car. He unlocked the car and grabbed Carmen by her arm. Cass pulled her close to him, making sure she wouldn't try to run. They walked to the opened door, and he walked her inside.

"Carmen, you got a couple choices right now . . . You could try to run and get shot"—he looked at the other female, and she flashed the 9 mm in her hand—"or you could be a good girl and do what you're told. Listen, you can make this a good thing or a very bad thing. It's up to you. This right here is Trini. She gonna make sure nothing happens to you unless you deserve it." He hoped his words were clear.

He reached into his pocket and pulled out a generous wad of cash and handed it to Trini. Then he turned around and walked out the door.

Carmen eyed Trini and knew she would kill on the spot if she made the wrong move.

Trini with her gun in hand walked in a circle around Carmen looking at her closely. "Don't worry, gal. I'ma tell ya how we doin' it," Trini said in a harsh manner, then opened a dresser drawer.

Carmen's eyes closed, and her legs began to shake. Urine trickled down her legs.

"Here a towel, rag, and a nightie. Go and wash ya rass," Trini said, motioning her to move quickly.

Carmen grabbed the stuff out of her hand and dashed into the bathroom, then locked the door.

Trini tapped on the door. "'Eh, gal, it don't have no window in there, you know," she said laughing.

Carmen got into the tub fully clothed, sat down, and bowed her head onto her knees. She sobbed, wishing she never met Cass. Her body began to rock. "How could you be so stupid?" she asked herself out loud. Her tears flowed uncontrollably. Carmen's future was now changed forever.

Cass was upset with himself as he hopped back into his ride. He rarely used his hands on women, but his frustration took over. He got back on I-94 and headed to Detroit with thoughts of Serenity on his mind. *I don't want to believe she's even capable of doin' that shit Shawn was sayin'! Damn, this bitch done know where I lay my head at, knows I get money . . . Damn! What the fuck a nigga 'pose to do!*

He made it back to Detroit and after thinking hard he called Iris.

"Iris, I need to see you."

"Hello to you too! It ain't gonna happen. I'm on my way to the airport. I have to take a trip to New York real quick, but I should be back in a day or two," she said stopping his demanding tone.

"Shit! Well, is there a later flight? I have to talk to you 'bout some shit." He knew of only one thing that could stop her from leaving. "It's 'bout some cash."

"If you can meet me at the airport in fifteen minutes, you will have five minutes to convince me," Iris blurted out and hung up the phone.

Cass stepped on the gas pedal. He pulled up to the airport in no time.

Iris stood waiting with her Gucci leather duffel bag. She saw Cass's car coming her way. She quickly looked at her watch to check the time. Cass drove up to her and got out of the car.

"All right, you got five minutes, starting now," Iris said pulling out a single Newport.

"I know you know Shawn P, correct?"

"Yeah, I do, but we don't get down like that anymore. So, what? He tryin' to take your prospects or somethin'?" Iris questioned carefully.

"Okay, do you know a chick named Serenity?" Cass asked.

"Continue," she said, not indicating her answer purposely. She took a pull off her cigarette.

"Well, Shawn stepped to me 'cause he heard some story about her setting up some big-time niggas back in D.C., and now she got almost a quarter mil' contract on her head." Cass continued, "He want me to set her ass up 'cause he know she been hangin' with me. He said something about it being easier. But he gonna toss me some green if I do. The only shit is, I got two days to get back to him or else she lies in a concrete bed without me gettin' paid. He only asked me if I wanted in because of the respect. You know me, I ain't no killa no more. Shit, I don't even handle guns anymore. But that money is callin' me. . . ."

"Cass, that's quite a story," Iris said as the wheels turned in her head.

"I want you—"

"Oh no, *you* didn't. I do what *I* say, not what you tell me to. Let me find out some things and I will call you in the morning. You look like shit! Go home. I'll hit you tomorrow," Iris said, plunking her cigarette butt into the street.

Cass looked at Iris wanting to continue their conversation, but he was quickly distracted when he heard a loud noise. He turned around to see someone had crashed into his parked car. He threw up his hands in frustration and yelled, "Fuckin' bitch!"

"Well, I see you gonna be doin' business for a while. We'll talk. Bye." Iris shook her head from side to side, then walked into the airport to catch her flight.

Chapter 16

"Take it in your mouth . . . Suck it . . . Yeah, I'm cumming . . . Yeah, get every drop, baby . . . Whoo-hoo!" Stuckey groaned. His body was weak from their nonstop, two-hour sex-a-thon.

"Stuckey, can I tell you somethin'?" Tootsie asked in a serious tone.

"Yeah, what?" he answered, still feeling fragile.

"I think Shawn P is going to kill me," Tootsie said with sadness in her voice. In actuality, she wasn't sure of what he would do to her after Serenity was taken care of.

"What the fuck you talkin' 'bout? That nigga hardly even talks to you. Most of the time, he tellin' me to tell you what to do!" Stuckey's voice grew louder. He stood up from the bed and walked to the window. His body became tense. He tried to hide any knowledge of the truth.

"But I have this feelin', and I thought about it. Why would he want me around after this shit goes down? He ain't been over here to say nothin' 'bout shit," Tootsie sat up.

"Tootsie, I'ma tell you somethin', but you ain't gonna like it, a'ight?" Stuckey turned around and looked at her. He hoped he was making the right decision on what he was about to say. "You a ho to him. He don't care nothin' about you. You already know that. Why you think he had you turnin' tricks for him when they let your ass out? He needed to break yo' ass down. Strip you of all happiness. I don't know shit, and I don't need to until it's necessary!"

"What you mean? I thought you—" Tootsie stood up and walked to him.

"Why you all up in my shit?"

"'Cause I'm scared! I mean, you don't fuckin' know what he gonna do. He got you and me here for like two months now. I know what you did back in D.C. You told me, you remember? What makes you think he ain't take your shit over and now plottin' for all of us to die?" She closed her eyes and braced herself for his slap across her face.

The slap never came.

"What the fuck you talkin' about?" His ears perked up.

"I'm just sayin', think about it, Stuckey. When was the last time you spoke to him?" She got bolder and turned her back to him. "That's why yo' ass—"

Stuckey's hand reached for the back of her neck. His grip tightened, and he whispered in her ear, "What you said, bitch?"

Tootsie went too far. Her eyes widened. "Baby, I didn't mean nothin' by it. I just want us to be together. I'm lucky I got you to look after me while I'm here." She kissed his lips softly.

"Get the fuck outta my room," he said almost in a whisper. His head was fucked up. *Tootsie is right. That nigga ain't come see me in a minute,* he thought. *Damn, could I be that blind?* Stuckey was tired of the street, but didn't want Shawn P to know he was getting out of the game. He reached for a single Newport and lit it. Then he grabbed his boxers off the floor and headed to the balcony. His mind continued to ramble back and forth while pacing and smoking. *Shit, now that I think about*

*it, he just might me tryin' to creep. He knows about my
connects when people need 'em big-ass choppers. Could
that be it? Does he know that I'm tryin' to get out? Is
he tryin' to take my source from me? When I took his
offer of two hundred stacks, I didn't expect to be here
this long. I should'a bounced when he gave me that fifty
stack. I could'a started my bubble real smooth with
that, but I ain't tryin' be in this shit no more.*

"Don't you want it?" Iris said.

"No, I really don't! My business with you is no longer!" Carla shouted.

"Whaaattt? Is that so?" Iris stood back and closed
her robe. "First of all, don't fuckin' yell. You can say
whatever you got to say without actin' like some nigga
from the street. Either you sit and talk or you leave.
'Cause trust me, you ain't the only business I got," Iris
said with a calm to her voice.

"A'ight, then let me ask you, how long you been traf-
fickin' pussy?" Carla asked without beating around the
bush.

"Um, what you talkin' about?" Iris asked, pretending
she didn't know the answer.

Carla chuckled lightly. "Did you think I wasn't gonna
find out? That shit wasn't gonna come back around to
me?"

"Carla, when this offer was put on the table to you,
you couldn't get nobody to fuck with you 'cause of your
sister's shit. And, I'm guessing you were already on
your last bit of dough. That's why you called me. You
scratch my back, I scratch yours. That's how it works.
There is no room for details. Details get you snitched
on or killed. I like my life. And, I'm sure you like yours,"
Iris said eyeing her.

Carla jumped up. "Wait! Hold up. I know you ain't tryin' to threaten me. I came here to make it clear to you. Your business is no longer mine. I ain't down with gettin' these bitches for you, then you sellin' them to rich-ass bastards out in other fuckin' countries for far more—"

"What, you want more money? Is *that* what this is all about? You could'a said that in the beginning," Iris interrupted.

"Hell, fuckin' yeah, I want more money. All 'em chicks you got from me I'm sure you made more than twenty-k. Don't think I'm stupid, Iris. The bitches I get you, they know they gonna be sellin' pussy or running drugs. You done went to the next level from what I hear. You snatch these broads up and sell 'em a false fuckin' dream. How they gonna be goin' places, and they ain't gonna be walking no street for tricks."

Carla shifted in her seat. "Basically, it's like this. Either you cut me in on the final payment, or I start opening my mouth. Don't get me wrong. I won't be snitchin', but I'ma make it harder for you to get that money."

"I see. Now you threatenin' me . . ." Iris stood up. "I think it's time you make your exit. I don't like when I'm backed into a corner."

"Backin' you into a corner? Nah, it ain't even like that. You didn't do your homework on me. Iris, you forget where I'm from; the capital of pimpin', Chi-town. One little brushfire can turn a forest black, just remember that." Carla stood up and walked out the door.

Who the fuck does this butch think she is? Could she really do that? I won't allow that shit! Iris's thoughts crammed her head.

***

"Carla, can you come and clasp this necklace for me?" Serenity yelled while she stood in front of the bathroom mirror and struggled to snap the costume jewelry around her neck. Her appearance was on point. A black Roberto Cavalli minidress and black peep toe pumps fit her shape nicely, accentuating her ass and thighs. Her hair was in a flat wrap with bangs, her makeup flawless. As soon as she added her accessories she would be perfect. She was excited to be stepping out as Cass's official girlfriend. He confirmed it.

"Damn, Serenity, I just walked in the door. Can't you wait a minute?" she asked feeling a little on edge after her meeting with Iris.

"Can you hurry up? Cass will be here any minute, and I don't want him waitin'. He's supposed to take me out to some exclusive club," Serenity said, still struggling to clasp the necklace closed.

Carla finally went up the stairs to help Serenity. "Wow! You look good. When did you get that?"

"Oh, Cass had it delivered to me today, along with these." Serenity showed off her new pumps.

"He did, huh? Well, make sure you tell him next time he wants to shop for you, then he gonna have to take you to Paris or Italy. Serenity, you gots to go big! Don't settle on little shit like this," Carla said.

"Damn, Carla, why you always think that way? Sometimes all this materialistic shit just doesn't matter. You mad 'cause you can't do it?" Serenity headed back to her room for her purse and phone.

"Yeah, okay. Now, you talkin' outta your asshole. If that nigga didn't have any money, you would not be on his arm," Carla said, not even addressing her insult.

"Carla, are you tryin' to get me mad? Or are you just mad that I actually got something to do and you don't?" Serenity walked past her and headed downstairs.

Carla followed behind her. "You mad 'cause I called your ass out? And you actually think just 'cause I haven't been shellin' out cash like I used to that somehow I'm jelly off of you. Serenity, you better check yourself in that mirror back upstairs," Carla said with a hard look on her face.

Serenity rolled her eyes. She heard her text message alert sounding off.

I'm outside.

"What the fuck is up wit' you, Carla? Is it 'cause I'm seeing Cass?" She walked to the front door.

"Yeah, I don't like that nigga. He too fuckin' ready to please all the fuckin' time! He reminds me of them pimps in Chi-town," Carla ranted.

"Now, you know you wrong for that shit! Carla, you don't know him or want to get to know him, for that matter. Every time I invite your ass to step out wit' us, you don't wanna come. You always got something to do! Get the fuck outta here wit' that shit!" Serenity's voice was loud.

"'Cause he ain't fuckin' worth me gettin' to know! That fool right there is pure show, nothing with substance. Shit, he says it's his place, but got his sister doin' all the real work." An ominous déjà vu feeling came over her.

"How you know 'bout his sister?" Serenity said in a mellow tone.

"Heaven is her name, right?"

"Yeah, so?" Serenity said, confident that Carla knew nothing.

"You know, when it's real late and you can't sleep so you stare at the ceiling? You can hear every giggle, the sound of the bed squeaking when you tossin' and turnin'. Well, I know you have a lot of conversations with that chick, that's all. Is there anything you might want to tell me?" Carla said, hoping Serenity would answer her suspicions.

"Why you always in my shit? Why you can't just leave me alone? Maybe I should just move out and get my own place." Serenity wanted to make sure Carla knew she had other options.

"Really? If that's how you feel, then fine. But make sure you know once you leave, your ass is on your own. I shouldn't even be listenin' to what you sayin' right now. You confused. You still don't even know if you like dick or pussy! So I sure as hell don't see you movin' out." Carla turned around and walked into the kitchen not saying another word.

"I gotta go. Bye," Serenity said, leaving with a bad feeling. Her sister's words affected her. She hated to argue with her sister knowing that all she only wanted was the best for her. Her stomach started to ache.

Carla's emotions and frustrations were coming to a head. Her sister didn't want to let her into her life. She just wanted to be left alone. Carla thought back on her earlier encounter with Iris. *Maybe I shouldn't of put her in such a hot spot. Shit, I wasn't gonna be a sucker. I know 'em girls is worth a lot more than ten Gs! The only way to let her know I mean business is to lay everything out on the table.*

Chapter 17

Cass sat in front of Serenity's house not sure if he could pull this off. Thoughts of Iris ran through his mind. *I hope she knows what she doin'. If this works, I'ma have some easy money to add to my stash. I'ma have to make that phone call now.*

He picked up his phone and dialed Shawn P's number.

"Yo, what's good, my nigga? I was wonderin' when you were gonna call me. You know you had less than twenty-four hours, right?" Shawn P's voice spoke.

"A'ight, you got a deal, but I want the money up front."

"Up front? Now what you take me for, a fuckin' fool? Listen, you get fifty Gs before and thirty after. Take it or leave it," Shawn P said.

"I'll take the fifty. I'll swing by your place in the morning. One." Cass hung up the phone unhappy that he couldn't get all the money up front. He looked out of his passenger-side window to see Serenity approaching. He quickly put a smile on his face and pushed the unlock button.

Serenity opened the door and hopped in. "Hey, baby," she said with a hint of sadness in her voice.

"What's wrong? Your sister actin' up again?" Cass asked.

"How you know? I just don't get it. Why she always showin' her face where it don't matter what she say?" Serenity reached for Cass's hand and squeezed it.

"Well, don't let her get you down. I have a special night planned, and it has only just started," Cass encouraged her.

"You're absolutely right. Now, where's this new club we goin' to? I think I'm gonna take a drink tonight," Serenity laughed.

"Really? Well, I better book a hotel room. Who knows how you gonna act! Listen, I just got to stop by the restaurant real quick; then we can be on our way." Cass turned the radio up and continued to drive.

Serenity lay her head on the headrest and stared out the window. *Is this what I really want? A man by my side? Why can't it be acceptable to have both? I don't want to give up what I have with Heaven.*

About thirty minutes later, they pulled into the parking lot of All Things Good.

"You want to wait in the car, or you want to come in?" Cass asked.

"Nah, I'll come in. Knowin' your ass, you'll be spinnin' around there for at least twenty minutes, so I might as well go chitchat with Heaven," Serenity replied.

"Yeah, you right. Come on." Cass opened his door, and then walked around to the passenger side to let Serenity out.

"Thank you." Serenity interlocked her fingers with Cass's. They headed toward the back exit to enter the restaurant.

Serenity knocked on Heaven's office door as Cass walked past her and went to his office.

"Come in," a voice said from behind the door.

Serenity walked into Heaven's office with a smile on her face. "Hey, Heaven, how you doin'?"

"Oh, just sitting here waiting for Rico so I can leave. He was supposed to be here like half an hour ago," Heaven said voicing her annoyance.

"Well, I could keep you company until Cass is ready. He came here for something. I don't know what's so important that we had to come here before we went out," Serenity said.

Heaven stepped closer to Serenity. She looked at her tight black minidress, admiring how well the dress fit her body.

Serenity took a seat, then pulled out her lip gloss. Her dress was so short that she felt a draft of air between her legs as she crossed them. Heaven ran her fingertip up Serenity's leg. Serenity tensed up immediately. Heaven's finger went higher and higher. Serenity was frozen in place as she felt Heaven's hand explore her body. It seemed like all of a sudden every nerve ending in her body was extrasensitive. Her body was on fire. Her mind was telling her to say "stop," and she formed her lips to say the words aloud, but Heaven's hands were so soft. Her touch was so enticing and gentle. Heaven was slowly inching her dress up. Now her entire lower half was bare with the exception of a lace black thong and her pumps.

Heaven's full lips pressed against Serenity's, and her fingers pulled her lace panties aside with expertise, exploring Serenity intimately. Her pussy was wetter than it had ever been. Her thong was soaked, and the smell of sweet cunt was in the air. The excitement of getting caught made Serenity bolder and want Heaven even more.

No one will know, Serenity thought. "No one will know," she whispered.

"I won't tell anyone, ma. I just want to make you feel good. Your pussy smells so good, Serenity," Heaven said. Her voice expressed her yearning. It was like she was an addict and Serenity's pussy was her drug of choice. Serenity's nipples were so hard that they were begging to be freed and sucked. The dark circles of her breasts were now pointed missiles standing sensitive and eager. Serenity gasped as she began to grind on Heaven's fingers.

"I don't want Cass to catch us, Heaven," she said, trying to ignore the feelings of pure goodness happening between her legs.

"The door automatically locks, Serenity. You need a key. Come on, don't make me stop now. Don't I make you feel good?" Heaven asked, not expecting an answer. Her long hair was partially in her face, and she stared directly into Serenity's eyes. She was so horny. Serenity's clit was throbbing.

Heaven motioned for Serenity to ease herself up onto the desk.

Serenity glanced at the door making sure it was shut. Her ass cheeks were hanging over the edge, leaving her pussy completely exposed.

Heaven stepped out of her own dress. Her clit was hard and eager. She stood in between Serenity's legs and pressed her body against her lover's. They were the same height, which allowed their bodies to align perfectly. Heaven rubbed her clitoris against Serenity's, causing her to cry out in ecstasy.

"Agh!" Serenity moaned as she humped furiously. "Yes!" The feeling was so intense. It felt better than any sex she had ever had with any man. Their pussies were so wet that they slid effortlessly against each other. The friction and pressure on her clit was almost painful it was so good. Serenity licked her lips as she watched Heaven's breasts bounce up and down. She grabbed one, then hungrily put it into her mouth.

"Ooh, shit," Heaven whispered.

The scent of sex was heavy in the air. "Let me taste your pussy," Heaven begged.

At this point, Serenity no longer protested. She just wanted Heaven to keep going. Heaven sucked her titties roughly, biting them a little bit. Serenity was trying to hold back her orgasm because she didn't want it to end just yet. Heaven's lips and tongue finally became acquainted with her love box. Serenity pumped her pussy into Heaven's mouth as she held her head in place, tightly against her legs. There was never a feeling so good; that, Serenity was sure of.

Serenity couldn't believe that she actually was doing this when Cass was so close by. All of a sudden, her tongue was extra wet. She wanted to taste Heaven. She pulled Heaven into her office bathroom, where she put her on the sink's edge and spread her legs wide. Heaven's wet, Brazilian cunt was glistening and smelled sweet. Serenity licked up the silky liquid flowing out of Heaven. It was nectar fit for the gods.

Heaven's office phone began to ring. She ignored it. The answering machine played out loud the incoming message.

"Heaven, it's me, Cass. This shit is packed, and Rico ain't even here yet. You're supposed to be running the show. Stop fuckin' around and get your ass out here!" The sound of Cass's voice brought Serenity back to reality.

"I can't do this," Serenity said. She stopped licking Heaven and started to pull her dress back down.

Heaven grabbed Serenity, brought her back into the office, and pushed her down on top of her desk. She pushed her dress back up and ripped her panties off. Heaven gripped her ass with one hand, licked her pussy with her tongue, and fingered her asshole simultaneously.

"Oh, I'm cumming!" Serenity called out in ecstasy. The muscles inside of her contracted, and she felt herself squirt as Heaven hungrily invited her release into her mouth.

"All I wanted to do is make sure you came and you wasn't shortchanged. I like our friendship. Whether it's talkin' late night on the phone or playin' with your sweet nana on the low. It really doesn't matter to me. Like I told you before, either way, my brother ain't gonna like what's goin' down." Heaven reached for her dress on the floor and slipped it on.

Serenity felt embarrassed and dirty, yet her pussy was still creaming at the thought of what had just gone down. She had masturbated plenty of times to the soft voice of Heaven, but when the opportunities of getting pleased by her came every so often, her body and mind were very acceptable to her infidelity. *It's not like we have an actual relationship,* she thought delaying her answer.

"You right," Serenity said shyly as she stood up. She brushed her hair back with her hand.

Heaven inched closer to Serenity, gliding her fingertips against Serenity's arms.

Suddenly the door opened. They both jumped. Serenity almost fell back onto the desk. Heaven looked at the door to see Cass walking in. She quickly scanned the room and saw Serenity's panties in plain view on the floor. She pretended to trip and scooped the lace panties up, then placed her hand behind her back.

"Heaven—What the fuck are y'all doin' in here? Serenity, come on, let's go. Heaven, get your ass out there 'til Rico get here." Cass looked at both of them and couldn't help but to smell a sweet scent permeating the room.

"Damn, Cass, it ain't like it's bumpin' or anything. Shit, I don't even think the band got here yet," Heaven said, trying not to look like she was busted.

"I'm sure your ass heard me over the answering machine. Stop playin'! Then again, you and Serenity can get so fuckin' loud with y'all yappin' and shit!" Cass let out a big laugh, not knowing how much he put everyone at ease.

Serenity walked up to Heaven noticing her panties in her hand. She stood beside her and grabbed the panties.

"Rico," Heaven yelled out.

This gave Serenity the opportunity for her to stuff her panties into her purse when Cass turned around.

"Rico, my man. Glad you're here! Maybe now some work can be done." Cass put his hand out for some dap from Rico.

"Ahh, whatever!" Heaven walked past, pushing through their handshake.

"Come on, Serenity, let's go," Cass said laughing.

Serenity and Cass walked to the exit door down the hall from Heaven's office. Cass's car was a few short steps away from the door. He unlocked the car doors and let Serenity in. He then walked around, hopped in, and pulled out of the parking lot.

Serenity walked into the club, and she immediately noticed the overabundance of female patrons. The ladies were three to one in comparison to the males, and there seemed to be a pulse of sexual energy throughout the place. There were dancers scattered on high-rise platforms and naked waitresses with body paint serving drinks. Girls were on girls mostly, and guys mingled and watched as the night's festivities took place. Serenity felt lost in the sea of bodies as she maneuvered her way through the crowd. She didn't know if Cass already knew about her true feelings for females. *Is that why he brought me here?* she questioned herself. She felt someone touch her waist.

"Follow me," Cass said, leading her up a set of wraparound stairs. She noticed a couple of girls in the club stalking her with their eyes, mean mugging as she went by. She stuck her middle finger up at one of the bitches who was watching her and continued to follow Cass into the VIP section. "I'm glad to see you liked my taste in clothes."

Serenity blushed and rubbed her hands across her flat stomach. "Thank you again. That was incredibly generous of you. I can pay you back."

"It was a gift, don't worry about it," he said.

She smiled as she admired his behind in his Armani slacks.

"What would you like to drink?" he asked, turning around with a smile.

She smiled back, and her face flushed. "I'll take a glass of chardonnay if they have it."

Cass quickly motioned the waitress over to place their drink orders. He looked over the balcony to see who was in the party. He could see a few females that he knew oh too well. He decided that this would be a short stay.

"Do you want to go down to the party and mingle for a bit?" he asked, hoping she wouldn't.

"I would rather stay here with you." She sashayed toward him, her long, toned legs crossing seductively as she closed the space between them. His eyes roamed her body, and the slight smirk on his face told her that he was pleased with what he saw.

"So why did you bring me here, Cass? This shit looks and feels like a strip club. I thought you were taking us to a party. This is far from a party. It's more like a place where you can buy and sell pussy. So tell me why we here?" she asked as she sat on his lap.

He laughed, his baritone chuckle low and sexy. "I thought you might want some foreplay before we head to the hotel to get our freak on. Haven't you ever heard of a threesome, ma?" he said playfully.

She punched him softly and rolled her eyes. "I know you ain't bring me here for that!" She jumped from his lap and stood up.

"I'm just fuckin' with you. We not stayin' here for long. I'm just here . . . Well, I'm what you would say a silent partner. I fronted the expenses and found the place, now I just wanna make sure shit is goin' well. And, the most important reason I brought you here is to show these females I ain't on the market! Besides, I don't want you to leave my side," Cass stated.

"I see . . . So why don't we just leave now so we can start our freak show?" Serenity had never been a ho, but tonight, she felt like she had something to prove to herself, as if being in that moment with Cass could erase what she did with Heaven.

She kissed him passionately, their tongues doing an erotic dance that made their temperature rise. His hands didn't roam. They graced her neck gently, lovingly. She could feel his dick growing. It felt so good she didn't want to stop, but they were surrounded by other VIP-goers.

"Wait—wait, we can't do this here . . . Can we?" she said as they came up for air.

"Ain't nobody watchin' us," he said. She was still on his lap and looked into his eyes. Their attraction was mutual, and she couldn't help but to kiss him again, this time lightly.

Serenity's head was all over the place. She liked Cass, yet that hadn't stopped her from having sex with his sister. It would be so wrong to even deal with him now. *What if he ever found out what happened?* she thought. *But I'm not gay. That was a mistake,* she reasoned.

Throwing caution to the wind, she kissed him and he invited it. This time, his hands explored with expertise, leaving trails of fire wherever he touched. She straddled him and grinded her hips onto his manhood to the sounds of Buju Banton. The shit felt so good to her. The lust and the pure excitement of getting fucked in a room filled with onlookers made her even hornier. She felt like she would explode just from dry humping him. Cass slipped his hand underneath her dress and was surprised she had no underwear on. His thick fingers entered her moist pink lips.

To Serenity, it was different than the sensation that Heaven had given her; less fulfilling in a way, but she accepted it all the same. Her moans and his heavy breathing filled her ears. She was more than ready.

"Come on, let's go to the bathroom. Follow me," he said quickly, rushing her through the oncoming crowd and into the bathroom. He took her into a stall and unzipped his pants. His manhood stood tall and thick. It was gorgeous.

"Do you have a condom?" she asked. She barely got the words out of her mouth before he was sliding one on. He entered her, and his stroke was so lovely, his grunts loud and strong as if he could barely contain himself.

"Yes, baby," she whispered in his ear as he lifted her leg. Just as the getting was getting good, he released one big moan.

"Oh shit," he whispered as she felt him release. They hadn't been fucking for ten minutes, and he was already a goner, leaving her with a soggy ass and a frustrated clit.

What the fuck? she thought. *This didn't happen before.*

He pulled out of her. She didn't want to say anything to embarrass him so she just remained silent.

"I'm sorry, ma. That shit was just too good," he said. He kissed her forehead.

She smiled halfheartedly and followed him out of the bathroom stall after fixing her clothes. *This nigga has everything—money, his own business, a nice car. He's good looking, and he is blessed in the dick department. He has the total package.*

Cass didn't bother to wait for her as he left the bathroom. He walked back into the VIP section and saw the waitress arriving with their drinks. He pulled out a hundred-dollar bill from his pocket, took a seat fully relaxed, and sipped his Grey Goose with cranberry.

Serenity took her time in the bathroom. She went back into the stall and pulled out a flushable wipe, then cleaned her vagina. She fixed her clothes and pulled out her panties from her purse and slipped them on. After that, she walked out of the stall and proceeded to wash her hands. *Damn, I wonder if he feels the same way I do. Can this even last?* she thought, allowing her hands to dry under the dryer. *I could use a man like Cass in my life. He's dependable and sweet,* so she thought.

Serenity walked out of the bathroom to see Cass conversing with another female. Her body immediately tensed. She wanted to stomp over there and tell that bitch to get out of her man's face before she put a stiletto up her ass. She watched Cass shake his head no and pointed in her direction. Her stilettos stabbed the ceramic tiled floor walking toward them. Before she reached them, the other female left with a look of pure hatred in her eyes. Serenity kissed his lips before she sat down. Cass handed her the glass of wine.

"No, I'm good. Don't feel like a drink anymore."

"I know you not gonna let that female upset you from havin' a good time with your man." Cass offered the glass again.

"From the looks of things, I think you told her who I was so I'm not worried about that, just so you know. Why don't we hit the dance floor and let me show these bitches what they *don't* have." Serenity grabbed Cass's hand and led him back downstairs.

As she walked through the club, she noticed that the intensity had gone from hot to scorching. A flashback of her rendezvous with Heaven entered her mind, but she quickly brushed it away. The crowd was too thick in the club, and the patrons were at full throttle by now. She felt molested by jealous eyes as she danced around Cass.

"Is that Cass's new bitch of the month?" she heard one girl say as she swished by.

"She'll be right here with us once her pussy is used up," another said.

Serenity rolled her eyes and thought, *I've got to get out of the range of these hating-ass bitches. It's time to go!* She couldn't wait to get out of the club, but she wasn't going anywhere without Cass close behind her. Her feet were starting to hurt, and it was beyond blazing in the club. It seemed like the later it got, the freakier the people in the club became. They walked by many sexual encounters. Bitches had no shame. Some were getting down, grinding, sucking, and damn near fucking niggas in the middle of the club without shame. They walked past the bar on their way out when Cass was stopped by some dude. She stood there impatiently as they talked. She was just ready to head to the crib and crash when she felt a hand tap her on her backside. She whipped around in irritation. The nigga in front of her was fine. Finer than fine, as a matter of fact, but she wasn't in the mood.

"Can I get a dance, baby girl?" She saw his lips move, but the music in the spot was so loud that she wasn't sure about what he said.

She stepped closer to him, and his breath reeked of liquor. He was so drunk it was seeping out of his pores. "I'm sorry. I didn't hear you. It's too loud in here," she said as she gave him her ear, leaning toward him so that she could hear him over the loud noises around them.

"What you drinking?" he asked.

She shook her head and replied, "Oh, no, thanks. I'm on my way out the door."

Serenity began to turn around to tap Cass when the guy pulled her back toward him. She rolled her eyes impatiently. She hated when niggas got drunk and rude.

"Come on, baby girl, have a drink with me. The night is young, baby. I want you to dance for me." He never released her upper arm and turned to the bartender. "Aye, let me get a Long Island and a Remy sour for the lady."

Serenity shook her head and spoke to the bartender, "No, cancel that. I'm leaving." She turned to the dude. "Can you let go of my arm now?"

The dude smiled slyly and whispered in her ear. "Loosen up, ma. I just want a dance from you, and if you're lucky, I'll give you some of this dick. My pockets are fat, baby girl. You know you want it."

He pulled her even closer, his grip on her arm getting tighter, then fondled her roughly with his other hand, squeezing her ass, then moving his hand upward until he had a feel of her breasts too.

Serenity smacked him hard across the face. "Mutha-fucka, do I look like a fuckin' stripper to you? Fuck a dance! What the fuck is your problem?" she demanded. "Loser-ass nigga!" she shouted.

"Bitch!" he mumbled angrily. He smacked the shit out of her, and the DJ instantly cut the music. Serenity felt her face getting red as a circle formed around them. The drunk pulled her toward him and threatened, "I'ma have fun fucking you up. I was willing to pay before. Now, I'ma take what I want."

Serenity struggled against him to get Cass's attention.

Cass stopped his conversation and turned in Serenity's direction. He stood up and faced this guy. "What the fuck you think you doin'?"

Both men stood face-to-face, about to square off. The patrons in the club didn't interfere, suspecting that it was a lover's quarrel. They just gathered around to watch the drama go down.

Out of nowhere, Cass knocked the drunk to the ground. "Yo, my man, what the fuck you doing, fam? You might want to say you're fuckin' sorry to her," he said. His voice was steady, and he was calm, but the look in his eyes let the dude know that he needed to take heed.

"Cass, man, my fault. I didn't know this bitch was taken. No disrespect, fam," he said. His angry tone was now a submissive one as he got up off the floor.

"You need to go sleep off that liquor, my man. Head out and get your head together." Cass then stepped closer to the guy so that Serenity wouldn't hear his next words. "The next time you see her, lower your head, nigga. You see all this pussy roaming around here? You've got to pay to play. This one is off-limits. Choose another bitch next time because if you ever touch her again, I'ma see you."

The dude scattered out of the club, and Cass put his arm around Serenity and squeezed her tightly. He whispered in her ear, "I'm sorry that happened. Next time, it won't be that pretty when another man lays his grimy hands on you. I'm sorry."

"Can we leave now?" Serenity whispered back.

The crowd began to disperse.

"Yeah, come on, let's go back to my crib, okay?" Cass grabbed her hand and led her out of the club.

Chapter 18

Serenity was shaken and rubbed her shoulders to soothe the goose bumps that had formed. If Cass hadn't intervened she didn't know what might have gone down. Niggas nowadays were so crass. She didn't know why dude had pushed up on her so disrespectfully, talking about paying her for dances and shit, but she wasn't the one. The situation could have easily turned ugly, and she sighed in relief that Cass had stepped in when he did.

"You all right?" he asked her while standing directly in front of her in his house.

She nodded and stepped closer him. He wrapped his arms around her waist as she placed her head on his chest.

"You're shaking," he whispered as he kissed the top of her head.

"I'm fine. It's not a big deal," she replied. She hadn't even realized that she was shaking. She just really wanted to sleep. "I'm exhausted. I just need to find a bed and forget about today." Cass thought she was referring to her confrontation with ol' boy, but she was referring to it *all,* including sex with Heaven.

"I really need to get my own place. That way, I can come and go as I please. I feel like a kid again. My sister been on some bullshit," she complained.

"Stay with me tonight," he suggested.

Serenity shook her head. "Nah, I'm good on that. Tell me, have you fucked any of those chicks in that club?" she asked.

"I'ma be honest with you. Yes, I have, but they just toys, nothing that would keep my attention. Maybe they see you as competition. You know, the new lady on the block that's coming to take their cash—I mean tryin' to take what they thought they could get," he added with a smile.

"I don't want nobody else's spot. If I got to take it, then it ain't mine from jump, so it'll be easy for the next bitch to steal it from me," she countered.

Cass laughed and nodded. He sat down next to Serenity. "You don't have to worry about no other chick checking you about me or coming at you wrong. If anybody does, I'll take care of it. Okay?"

"Okay," she agreed. "You're really a good guy, aren't you?" she asked. He was sweet, and she liked him. *Maybe my pussy is just that good,* she thought with a smirk.

"Nah, not really. I don't claim that good-guy shit," he flirted. "Chill out here. I gotta go take off these slacks and shit. I'll be back. Help yourself to anything in the kitchen."

Serenity sat down on the leather sofa, and before she knew it, she was out like a light. Cass came back to find her fast asleep. He scooped her up and placed her in his bed. He lay next her, not wanting to give her up. He thought about the past two months. *Now if Shawn P ain't never offered me money, she probably would be wifey! Damn, can I do this? Do I want to do this? With the money I'm getting from the strip club, restaurant, and chicks I be gettin' to Iris, shit, I'm fuckin' good! But damn, I want more! Shit, I got 'til tomorrow before this shit go down. Fuck!*

When Serenity awoke, she was in a plush room, and her body felt like it would sink deep into the luxurious bedding and pillows. She knew where she was.

She arose from the bed still wearing the freak 'em dress Cass had chosen for the club. She walked out of the room in search of Cass, but he was nowhere to be found. She took it as an opportunity to snoop through his things since the last time she was in such a rush to talk to Heaven.

She quickly went into the bathroom. She knew if there was a woman in his life, that would be the place where her presence would be most felt. She knew game, and it always started out with leaving perfume, deodorant, and little products like that behind, but as Serenity nosily opened his medicine cabinet, all she saw was Cass's stuff. "I know this nigga be fucking around as fine as he is," she whispered. She decided to check his room, and when she turned around, she saw Cass leaning against the bathroom door, watching her.

"Shit!" she exclaimed with her heart jumping in her chest. "You scared me!"

"You find what you looking for?" he asked with a smile.

"I uh—was looking for Tylenol. I have a headache," she lied, unconvincingly. "Where'd you go?" she changed the subject.

"Come on," he said as he led her to the kitchen. When Serenity entered, the table was set with blueberry pancakes, eggs, bacon, and biscuits. A feast fit for a queen. His queen. "I hope you hungry."

Serenity nodded. "Starving," she answered.

The two enjoyed breakfast, talking and laughing with each other. He fed her; she fed him. They clicked instantly, and when he leaned in to kiss her, she kissed him back. He put her on top of the table, spreading her legs, and to his surprise, she was wearing panties. He couldn't remember having to remove her underwear when they were in the club. He quickly shook it off and slipped his finger inside her.

She had been so disappointed with his sex game earlier; she hoped he'd redeem himself now because she had a big juicy nut building in her pussy. Cass's penis grew, and he pressed his hardness against her stomach.

"It's so big," she whispered in his ear. "Can I taste it?"

"Yeah, ma, suck it for daddy," he urged.

She got on her knees and opened wide as she grabbed his shaft and licked the tip of his dick. His balls were tight and large, which turned her on. She fingered herself while sucking him off. Cass was moaning so loud that she said, "Don't nut, Cass. I want some of that big dick inside me."

He was thrusting into her mouth, and she was taking his entire eleven inches, releasing her throat muscles so that she wouldn't gag. The scent of him was so sweet, and surprisingly, this time, he was controlling his orgasm. She figured it must have been a onetime thing and continued to please her new man. She wrapped her hands around his shaft, put saliva all over it, and twisted her hands in different directions as her tongue caressed him. His knees wobbled.

"Damn, ma, ooh, shit. You're the best," he moaned as he gripped her head. He was straight fucking her face, but she didn't mind. She was working her own fingers on her pussy like her life depended on it. As she fingered herself she thought of Heaven. She worked them faster.

"Mmmm," she mumbled, causing Cass to feel vibrations on his dick. She put his balls in her mouth. He was really bringing the freak out of her, and she loved it. He was hairless and fresh smelling, so her tongue explored everywhere.

"Serenity, stop, baby. I'm about to nut," he begged, his voice rough and strained, yet he was still gripping the back of her head.

"You almost there?" she asked.

"Yes, ma, shit!" he screamed like a bitch. Serenity was literally blowing his top, giving him the best head he had ever received.

"You gon' beat this pussy, Cass?" she asked. She stopped sucking and waited for his answer.

"Hell, yeah, ma, but keep sucking," he moaned. She gave him another long, hard suck.

"You gon' make me cum, Cass?" she asked.

"Yeah, ma," he promised.

"You want me to swallow it, baby? Is it sweet?" she asked, referring to the cum that was threatening to ooze out of his tip at any moment.

This time he couldn't respond. Serenity had him in a zone. "If you fuck me good, baby, I'll swallow it all," she promised. She stood up with her pussy throbbing and ready to be pounded and turned around so that she was leaning over the table.

He didn't hesitate to spread her legs. He rubbed his dick against her wetness and spread it over her asshole. He was circling his tip against it, wetting her anal opening and turning her on. She had never had a nigga go in her ass. She had heard that the shit hurt worse than life, but the way her body was feeling, she was open to try any freaking thing he threw at her. She wasn't going to invite him in, but if he took it there, she wouldn't stop him.

"I'm just gon' put the tip in, ma. If I go in this pussy right now, I'm gonna nut," he whispered. He inserted his penis into her asshole slowly. She tensed up. "Just relax," he urged. She released her muscles and inhaled as he got the tip in. That shit made her clit harder. She felt him stroke his shaft while the tip was in her ass. She couldn't take it anymore. She had to get hers. She felt like an unrestrained fiend. She was so horny, and she needed his dick just that bad.

"Cass, put it in, baby. Fuck me," she begged.

Cass removed his dick and shoved it into her pussy, filling it up. He lifted her hips and the first stroke put her in bliss. Their moans were loud, and his strokes were deep and firm, just like she liked it. He was killing it, but not even twenty strokes in, he was pulling out and shooting his seed all over her ass and back. Her cunt was aching because she hadn't gotten hers. He had lasted so long while she was sucking his dick, but as soon as he got inside her, he was a goner. She was frustrated, and her clit was protesting by throbbing. She had to relieve the pressure or that orgasm would fuck with her all night. Cass turned her around and kissed her passionately, with his hands roaming her body.

Serenity smiled. She was disappointed, but there was something about that man. He gave her butterflies in her stomach; he made her clit tingle and swell; he even made her feel like his queen.

"That was good, ma," he said. He picked her up all the while kissing her and making her feel special. He looked in her eyes. His gaze was so sincere. He instantly melted her heart. "I want you to stay here with me, Serenity. I'm feeling you. I want to take care of you."

How could I be mad at him for wanting to keep me for him? He's good in bed . . . or at least when he wants to be. He barely knew her. In fact, he didn't know her, but she could see it in his eyes that he was smitten.

But her clit was still throbbing.

It was still lonely.

She was still craving fulfillment.

"Cass, I can't—We only been seeing each other for a short while, and besides, this is the only the second time I've been to your house. You like my company, but that don't mean we're supposed to live together, Cass. It's too soon," she said, still in his arms.

"Shh," he whispered. "I'm a grown man, and I know what I want, Serenity. Yeah, it's soon, but I'm feeling you. I want you, ma. Fuck all the bullshit. I'm not a young nigga no more. I know it's gon' be days that you gon' get on my fucking nerves. And, I know it's gon' be days that will be hard, but I want it, ma. I want you. I don't give a fuck about any other bitch, Serenity. These bitches don't stimulate me like you do. I love the way my name sounds rolling off your tongue, baby. If it don't work out, then we'll both move on, but right now, today, I want you, Serenity"—he stopped to kiss her—"I want you."

"I want you too, Cass," she replied, and she wasn't lying. She really did want his ass. At that moment she wanted him to make her cum more than she wanted to breathe air. The way he spoke to her, the way he commanded her attention, the way he made her want to follow his lead was pulling her in, but what was she going to do when she wanted him to beat her pussy up? She could feel her heart beat in her clit. She tightened her thighs to apply pressure to it. She told herself that she was going to masturbate as soon as Cass went to sleep.

"Say you'll stay," Cass urged.

"I'll stay," she answered with an unsure smile. The chemistry between them was electric. She had never felt the way that Cass made her feel, but all new relationships were fiery, spontaneous, and fun. She didn't want to confuse that attraction or lust for more than what it was, but he was persistent, and she would give it a try. She let out a big sigh.

"You're so beautiful, Serenity," he whispered.

"Why do you want me here?" she responded, sitting up. "Is this just a sex thing?" she asked aloud.

He laughed at her and replied, "No, 'cause it took me at least two months to get it. And, now that I got it, ma, a nigga can't fuckin' stop! Know what I mean?"

He picked her up, carried her into the bedroom, and was still planting kisses all over her.

Normally, Serenity would have loved all of the attention, but tonight, it was just making her hot and bothered. The way Cass touched her made her want to fuck, not slow and intimate, but fast and rough. She just wanted to *fuck* him. He ran his fingers down her body, causing a pool of wetness to form between her legs. She sat up and wrapped her arms around his neck, then pulled him down on top of her. They had sex again. It was passionate and heartfelt, but again, he didn't rock her until she came. Instead, she satisfied him and put him to sleep.

When she heard him snoring lightly from his side of the bed, she opened her legs and stuck her middle and index fingers inside as she stroked her clit with her thumb. She pinched her nipple with the other hand as she rotated her hips, making love to herself, pleasing herself the way she used to in college when she would hear her suitemates next door having orgies. She closed her eyes and imagined Heaven between her legs. She was moving her hips and plunging her fingers in her wetness so hard that she had to bite her lip to keep from moaning aloud. The shit felt good. She remembered the orgasm that Heaven had bestowed upon her. She remembered Heaven's mouth on her pussy and how good it felt. She pulled her fingers out and put them to her lips, then sucked her own juices off of her hands.

"Mmm," she moaned, unable to help herself. Her pussy was sweet like honey. She needed to feel a tongue between her legs. She wished it could be Heaven's. She was frustrated, and no matter how much she worked on her clit, she couldn't get the kind of orgasm that she was chasing. She had so much sexual frustration built up from Cass's shortcomings. She had to get hers. She sat up in bed and looked over at Cass. He was sound asleep. She straddled him and sat her butt on his chest. Her neatly groomed palace was in his face. He opened his eyes and smiled. "What you doing, ma?"

"Eat it, Cass. I need you, baby," she whispered.

Cass dived right in. He held her plumb ass in his hands and French-kissed her southern lips as she rode his face. His face was covered with her juices as she threw her pussy at his lips like a ho in heat.

"Suck it, Cass. Pull on my clit," she demanded. She wanted to feel like she had with Heaven, and although the feeling wasn't exactly the same, it would do. It took her close to the place she wanted to be. She closed her eyes and rode his juicy tongue as he stuck it inside her hole. "Ohh, shit, baby, yes!" she screamed in pleasure as she felt her orgasm build. She was so sensitive down there by this point that when he finally pulled the orgasm out of her, she squirted. A smile spread across her face, and she slid off of him. She went into the bathroom and got a warm towel to clean herself with. She then took a towel to Cass and wiped his face.

"I can get used to that, ma. Wake a nigga up like that too many times and I'ma try to wife you," he said with a laugh. He pulled Serenity close, and finally, she was able to go to sleep satisfied, but Heaven lurked in her dreams.

I can't stop the images in my head. I want her badly. Nobody has ever made me feel like that. Shit, not even Sadie.

Cass didn't want Serenity's destiny shattered. He was now really starting to like her. He made up his mind. But he might lose everything—his money, lifestyle, and the only family he had, Heaven.

Chapter 19

"Wake up, lady," Cass said as he got on his knees so that he was eye level with Serenity. "It's about seven in the evening. We been fuckin' and sleepin' since we came in last night."

She didn't stir, and he stared at her smooth skin for a few seconds before calling her again. She was so beautiful to him, one of the most intriguing females he had ever met, and although he wasn't in love with her, he did enjoy being around her. *I don't think I can do this! Shit! Fuck! Well, I took fifty grand from the nigga already, so fuck him! I don't got no loyalty to him!* he thought, wishing that she hadn't brought him to his knees for the last several hours.

Serenity yawned and stretched her arms above her head before finally noticing he was trying to wake her.

"You're gonna have to get your things from your sister's place at some point. But for now, I can provide you with everything you need. Here's my Amex," Cass said as he stood to his feet.

"Where are you going?" she asked while taking the card out of his hands.

"Over to the restaurant. I gotta do a few things," he replied.

"You were serious about me moving in?" she asked skeptically.

He nodded. "Of course, I was. If you hurry, you can still make it to the mall and pick up a few things, or go to your sister's and grab some of your stuff. I went out earlier and made you a copy of my house key. It's on the kitchen counter."

Serenity felt like she was in a whirlwind situation. The shit was moving extremely fast. She was being swept off of her feet, but she didn't want Cass to think she was a gold digger or even worse, a ho.

"Cass, is all this okay? Are you sure about this?" Her tone was uncertain, and Cass stepped back into the room, then sat on the edge of the bed. His hand touched her face, then slid down to her shoulder where he massaged it gently. He pulled her toward him so that their foreheads touched.

"Just trust me, a'ight? Put your trust in me, ma. I'm sure," he said before kissing her softly.

Everything he said seemed to be the right thing. Everything he did was right on time. He made her comfortable in his presence. Serenity liked him. She couldn't help but to admit that. He only seemed to be lacking in one area so far; he couldn't make her nut like she wanted. Serenity told herself that she would be a fool to fuck up a good thing for such a dumb reason.

Cass got up and walked out of the room. "I'll see you later. Just call me when you're ready. You can use my other car in the garage," he said, then disappeared out of the room.

She didn't move until she heard the front door close. Then she walked around his crib as if it were hers, enjoying the feel of the plush carpet between her toes. She looked around the home and smiled. *If the nigga want me to move in here, then who am I to say no?* she thought. *I'm tired of my sister always in my shit anyway!* She hurried to her phone to call her sister.

"Carla," she said.

"Serenity, where you at? Your car is still here," Carla said in a low voice.

"We need to talk. I'm moving in with Cass." Serenity listened for a response.

"What? Just like that? You don't even know dude," Carla ranted.

Serenity rolled her eyes and put her hand on her hip as she cradled the phone in between her ear and collar bone. "Yeah, he asked me to stay with him, and yeah, I said yes. Let me guess—you got a problem with that, don't you?" she asked.

"You don't need to be living with Cass, Serenity," Carla said in a defeated tone, knowing her sister already made up her mind.

Here we go, Serenity thought. "Why? Because you won't be able to control who I see and what I do?" she asked with an attitude.

"You know you wrong 'cause I ain't never stopped your ass from doing or seeing whoever you wanted—" Carla started to respond, but Serenity cut her off.

"Carla, stop hating all the fucking time. The more time I spend with Cass, the more you start actin' funny, like you don't want me around him. I'm moving in with him. I'ma grown-ass woman, and I can do whatever I want to do. So do me a favor and stop being so fucking overprotective and be happy for me," Serenity spewed. She hung up the phone, tired of her sister's animosity. Once she got dressed quickly, she grabbed her keys and headed out the door. Carla hadn't done anything but make her want to stay with Cass more, just to piss her off.

Carla couldn't believe what she just heard. *How could she be so fuckin' dumb? She movin' in with this nigga? Now I definitely got to find out more about this nigga!* Carla's mind was blaring with negativity. She had to shake her mind off of Serenity and concentrate on her next move. She looked at her phone, then dialed Iris's number. "Hey."

"Carla, I was wondering when you were gonna call me," Iris answered.

"Well, have you thought 'bout what I said?" Carla cut straight to the point.

"Yeah, I have, and I don't think it would be a good idea for you to open your mouth about nothing. Listen, you really don't want to get on my bad side. This game that I play can end up causing you a lot of pain. And . . . It won't be just physical either," Iris stated in a cold tone to make her point clear.

"You think so, huh? I guess—"

"You thought you could scare me into giving you more money. Now that you know that ain't gonna work, what you gonna do now 'cause you gave me enough time to blacklist yo' ass to everyone within a hundred-mile radius. So whatever money you got you better hold on to it 'cause who knows where you gonna get yo' next stack from. You better go get a job, bitch!" Iris hung up the phone enjoying her rant.

Carla sat there fuming. She didn't think Iris would move so quickly. She just fucked up the easiest money she could have gotten. Now she didn't know what to do. It wasn't like she could call her back and pretend the whole thing was a joke. *Damn, my sister is leavin', and I can't change shit about it unless this nigga Cass outta the picture. Now I just fucked up my money. What the fuck a bitch 'pose to do now? Fuck!*

Serenity hopped into Cass's Lexus and pulled out. She didn't know exactly when she and Carla went their separate ways, but a part of her wanted the companionship of her sister. Then again, the other half of her said, "Fuck it!" They were both stubborn, and neither would ever make the first steps to fix whatever was wrong between them. Serenity didn't like how Carla was so resistant to Cass. It was like he was water and she was oil.

Serenity arrived just before eight at Carla's. She pulled out her key and fitted it into the keyhole. When she entered the house, she could smell weed throughout. Carla has never smoked in the house before, and this put Serenity on edge. She tried to pay it no mind and walked up to her room without calling out her sister's name. Serenity wanted to avoid her in every way possible. In the room, she grabbed her suitcase out of the closet. *All of my things are not gonna be able to fit in just one suitcase. Shit, Carla has my other one!*

She hesitated at first, but she admitted to herself that grown women do grown things. Serenity headed downstairs, stood outside the bedroom door, and took a deep breath before knocking on it. "Carla, you alone?"

"Yeah, why wouldn't I be? What's the problem?" Carla asked in a low voice. She put out the blunt in the ashtray. "Sorry, I didn't know that you were comin' home. I know how much you hate smoke in the house. So I guess you here to get some of yo' stuff, huh?"

"Carla, it doesn't have to be like this. Cass is good to me and for me. He cares for me. He wants nothing but good things for me. Why can't you see that?" Serenity pleaded with tears beginning to form in her eyes.

"Don't get too caught up in Cass. He can have his pick of any woman in Detroit, so don't think he's going to be faithful to you. He's always looking for the new hot thang," Carla said. "What makes you think he so good for you?"

"Um," Serenity groaned as if the conversation was hurting her head. "Why, Carla? Why are you trippin' 'bout me and Cass? Do you know something I don't? Do you just not *want* to see me happy?"

"I'm just trying to put you up on game so you won't be left looking stupid. Cass, like every other nigga out here, he tryin' to go legit without leavin' the streets. All that can lead to is problems. Don't let him suck you into his storefront reality," Carla spewed. "He don't only own that restaurant, but he owns one of the busiest strip clubs in Detroit," Carla said thinking that it would put a shock to her system.

"Tell me something I don't know. And so what if he's had a lot of bitches? You really don't know that for sure. Well, he only got one right now, and that's me. That's all I'm concerned about," Serenity replied. "I just want my suitcase that you used. Then if you need to reach me, you know where I'll be," she huffed.

"Are you fuckin' serious? You know what? Sometimes you just got to stand clear out of the way in order for folks to grow," Carla spoke in a stern, calm voice, retrieving the suitcase from her closet.

"Thank you," Serenity replied, taking the suitcase, then headed out of the room. She held on to the suitcase tightly as she walked back up the stairs. Quickly, Serenity emptied her closet and dresser drawers as much as she could to fit into the suitcases.

Soon after, Carla could hear Serenity dragging her suitcases down the stairs to the front door. She sat on the edge of her bed listening to every thump and fighting the urge not to go stop her.

Serenity lugged her two heavy suitcases out of the house to the car. She placed them into the trunk, then sat in the car. She prayed that Carla would come around and be happy for her. Serenity wanted to go by the restaurant just to pop up on Cass to prove Carla was wrong but decided on going straight to his house instead.

As she drove into Cass's driveway, she saw Heaven stepping out of her car, looking as if she'd just stepped out of a fashion magazine. Serenity looked around to see if Cass was with her. *Why is she here?* she wondered. Serenity's palms began to sweat, and her heartbeat sped up as she got out of the car.

"Hey, Serenity, I'm sorry. Cass told me what happened in the club last night," Heaven said.

Serenity's heart was racing, and she didn't know how Heaven could be so cool and collected, as if nothing had ever happened between them. Her eyes focused on Heaven's glossy lips, and she shifted nervously. Turning, she popped the trunk open to retrieve her suitcases.

Heaven smiled. "It's okay. It doesn't have to be weird between us. It's not a big deal, and I don't want you to be uncomfortable around me," Heaven said as she rubbed Serenity's arm.

Serenity inhaled. Every time Heaven touched her, she melted, no matter how subtle. "I . . . uh," Serenity stopped herself from stuttering and took a deep breath. She felt like a bumbling teenager who was talking to her crush for the first time. She smiled and shook her head. "It's a little weird."

"Let me help you with that." Heaven reached for the smaller suitcase. "You found a place already?" Heaven asked.

"Well, not exactly. I'm moving in with Cass. He offered, and I agreed. I just hope it was the right decision," Serenity said. She didn't know if Cass mentioned her shacking up with him. She was Cass's girl, but for some reason, she felt funny telling Heaven.

"So you're Cass's girl, huh?" Heaven asked.

"We're . . ." Serenity tried to find a way to say it, but when she couldn't substitute the words she finally admitted, "Yeah, we're together."

Heaven nodded. "Cass and I always did have the same taste." She turned and walked away in her yellow Gucci sundress which complimented her skin as her matching heels kissed the ground. She pulled the suitcase to the door and waited for Serenity to catch up.

Serenity thanked God that there hadn't been any drama and wondered how she was going to handle the situation with Heaven. *Should I tell Cass what happened between us?* she thought. She quickly decided against it. He wouldn't understand and would probably look at her completely differently. *It's not like I'm lying to him. After all, what he doesn't know can't hurt him.* She picked up her cell and called him.

"Hey," he answered. "Did you go shoppin'?"

"No, I actually just went to my house and packed some suitcases. I'm going to drop them off at your house, and then grab something to eat," she said.

"A'ight, ma, I gotta go," he suddenly replied before hanging up the phone.

Serenity shoved her phone into her purse and wrestled her suitcase out of the trunk, then proceeded to the front door. She opened the door and entered her new home. As soon as she shut the door, Heaven walked up behind her.

"Let me suck on your pussy," Heaven whispered seductively into Serenity's ear.

Heaven's command made Serenity instantly wet.

"Heaven, what are you doing? You know I'm with Cass. He's your brother, and I'm not trying to play games to fuck anything up," Serenity said, but even as she protested, Heaven opened her legs wide and guided her fingers to stroke her waiting clit.

"I don't want to talk about Cass, Serenity. I just want to make you cum. And from the looks of it, you *want* to cum."

"Yes," she answered against her better judgment. She was playing with fire. The first time she'd slept with Heaven had been a mistake, but now she was inviting her. She wanted to, or more truthfully, she couldn't help herself.

"Cass can't make you cum like me, Serenity. He can't lick and eat your pussy like I can. I'm wet as hell just being so close to you. I want you to feel it," Heaven whispered. Her voice was smooth and sexy.

Serenity worked her clit and inserted two fingers inside her hot flesh while Heaven pressed her body against Serenity's. Now Serenity was against the wall with her back still to Heaven. "Is it wet, Serenity?"

"Uh-huh," she moaned.

"How wet?" Heaven asked.

"It's *real* wet," Serenity answered. "Oh shit, it's drippin'."

"Is it sweet?" Heaven asked. "Taste your fingers and tell me if it's sweet," she instructed.

Serenity did as she was told, lifting her fingers to her mouth and sucking the juice from them.

"Mmm, it's sweet. . . . My pussy is throbbing," Serenity whispered. Her nipples ached, and she wanted to pinch them so badly. She wanted to turn around and have Heaven's mouth full of her flesh. The thought of Heaven's tongue playing with her wet pussy caused miniorgasms to go off as she gyrated her ass against Heaven. She wanted more. She needed to cum, preferably inside of Heaven's mouth. She promised herself that she would never take it that far with Heaven again, but this girl did something to her. Heaven made her feel like no other. She was slowly becoming addicted to her sex.

Serenity had always been a closet freak. She had sex with Rock in a Macy's dressing room when they went shopping one time. It was like when she wanted to cum, she'd do anything to get it, but orgasms received from a woman were so much more intense. She didn't know if it was because of all the sneaking around she was doing with Heaven, but all Serenity knew was that she didn't want to stop it.

"I want to taste it," Heaven whispered. "My clit is so juicy, Serenity. It's so fat and wet. You want me to stop or you want me to keep talking?" she asked.

Serenity turned around and walked to the sofa. She sat down, then spread her legs wide open pulling her bright pink thong to the side. "No more talking," she moaned.

"You want me to fuck you, Serenity?" Heaven asked. "Tell me you want me to fuck you."

"I want you to fuck me," she said as she rolled her clit in between her thumb and forefinger.

Serenity was rolling her hips and palming her pussy when Heaven kneeled on the floor in perfect position to feast. "Shit!" Serenity cried out as Heaven's tongue slowly circled her inner thigh and snaked her way to her ripe peach.

Serenity grabbed Heaven's head and guided her to her face. All of Serenity's reservations went out the window as they tongued each other sensually. Only the thin fabric of their dresses separated them, and Heaven's fingers were already inside Serenity as she opened her legs wider. Their breathing was heavy and labored.

"We shouldn't be doing this," Serenity whispered as she grabbed Heaven's plump behind and rubbed it gently. She closed her eyes as she felt her clitoris gorge in wanton excitement. Her sexual desires were too strong. Cass couldn't fuck her the way she wanted to be fucked. She wanted to be fucked long and hard. She wanted to be fucked like a whore, and it was the bad side of her that was telling her that this was all right.

"You've been thinking about me since last night," Heaven said assertively. "My brother doesn't know what to do with you. You like pussy, Serenity; there's no denying it."

Heaven took Serenity's hand and led her upstairs. Serenity didn't resist, even though she knew she was dead wrong. The excitement of fucking Heaven in Cass's bed made her want it even more. She had never felt like this with any man. She was beginning to think that she yearned to be with a woman all along, even if it did get her in a hot mess before. She was in the actual act of lesbianism again, and she liked it. She loved it. She *needed* it.

Serenity lay down on the bed, and Heaven removed her panties, then dove in between her legs, lapping up her special mixture as if it were a world-class, five-star cuisine. Heaven's tongue was so hot, and Serenity's grinding made it feel so right. The sin of it all felt so good. Heaven smiled as she crawled seductively up Serenity's body. She straddled Serenity, her panty-less pussy rubbing against Heaven's.

Heaven's clit was throbbing, and Serenity could feel the pulse against her own. Each little thump was threatening to take Serenity over the top. Heaven pulled her dress up over her head. She was now nude. Her plump and firm breasts were perfect. The dark nipples contrasted against her light skin. The room was silent as Heaven removed Serenity's dress. They admired each other.

"You're gorgeous," Heaven whispered as she arched her back and lowered her head so that she could devour a nipple. She cupped Serenity's breasts and sucked like a baby thirsting for milk.

"You make me feel so good," Serenity whispered.

Heaven sat back up. Straddling Serenity, she began to move her hips.

"Ohh," Serenity moaned.

Heaven rode Serenity's clit like a jockey, creating friction between them. She pulled her pussy lips back so that her pearl was fully exposed, and then continued to grind.

"Ohh, Serenity," she moaned. Heaven had never experienced many encounters with other women, but Serenity's cunt was so wet and sweet. Heaven enjoyed femme lesbians. She wanted someone soft and gentle to rub on, to suck on, to be on, and Serenity fit her preferences to a tee. Serenity's pussy was like a peach, and she was rotating her hips as if her life depended on it. Serenity bucked back, and then reached up, grabbing a handful of titties.

"I want to taste you," Serenity admitted.

Heaven sat up. She stopped moving.

Serenity's tongue was salivating at the mere thought of it.

Heaven turned on her back, and Serenity climbed on top. She brought her face close to Heaven's southern lips and inhaled deeply. *Damn, her shit smells so good,* she thought. Serenity had thought she was over her curiosity, but strangely, she felt a strong sense of attraction to women. It was almost natural to her. Heaven's womanhood was pretty and neat; her lips were swollen in anticipation. Heaven had a fatty, and it was wet and glistening—inviting. Just as Serenity was about to wrap her lips around that luscious-looking clit, she heard her phone. She ignored it. She swallowed Heaven's clit with intensity. They both moaned loudly, enjoying each other's touch and taste.

***

Cass headed home after talking to Serenity. He wanted to surprise her since she didn't expect him until later that evening. He pulled into the driveway, cursing his sister for her poor parking skills making it impossible to drive into the garage. He grabbed a small bag from the passenger seat before exiting the car. *Hopefully, this will give her some security after I tell her who's gunning for her,* he thought as he walked to the front door. He slipped the key into the keyhole and turned the doorknob. Upon entering, he saw two suitcases and two purses beside them. He thought he heard moaning but told himself that it was probably the TV.

Cass stood still when he heard Serenity's voice yelling, "Yeah, make me cum . . ." He walked quietly to the staircase leading up to the second floor. He could hear sexual moans. "Oh, I know this bitch didn't think she could fuck another nigga in my house, let alone in my fuckin' bed!" Cass said, looking at the bag in his hand. He pulled out a white box and opened it. He gripped the hard steel of a 9 mm, then inserted the loaded clip. Then quietly, he inched up the stairs, fuming with anticipation. The moans got louder.

He reached his room but wasn't prepared for what he saw. His room door was wide open, and he could see Heaven's head moving between Serenity's legs. His gasp wasn't heard over their loud groans of ecstasy. He stood in the doorway watching how Serenity's body shook from her climax. He didn't want to believe that the girl he was just about to give his life up for was fucking his sister. It instantly solidified his gut feeling about Heaven; she was gay.

He stepped out of the doorway and leaned against the wall. *This fuckin' bitch! And she got my sister involved with her cunning, fuckin' ways. Fuck that. I don't give a fuck about this bitch no more! As for my sister, I'ma handle her ass after Serenity is gone.* Cass's thoughts quickly jumped back and forth. He took a deep breath and tiptoed back down the stairs. He walked to the front door, opened it, then slammed it shut. Immediately afterwards, he walked into the kitchen and opened a bottle of Patrón. He stashed the 9 mm in one of the kitchen drawers.

"Oh my God, it's Cass! He's home!" Serenity said in a panic. They jumped up and rushed to dress. Serenity's eyes were filled with fear.

Heaven grabbed an air freshener from his bathroom and sprayed the room, then opened a window so that the smell of pussy could dissipate. She straightened the bed and said, "Be calm and stop looking so guilty. He'll never know." Heaven winked, and then exited the room.

Cass could hear the rustling upstairs. "I'm in the kitchen," he shouted.

As Heaven and Serenity were descending the stairs, Serenity froze. Her nerves made her feel nauseated, and her stomach threatened to blow at any second. She felt like her guilt was written all over her face. Apprehensively, she straightened her dress.

"Hey, big bro," Heaven greeted, keeping her cool as she waltzed into the kitchen. Her expression was innocent, and her performance was Oscar-worthy. She reached for a glass from the cupboard and poured herself a drink.

Serenity was shaking in her boots. She was sure that Cass could see right through her. She felt transparent and was waiting for the accusations to start flying. She took a deep breath and waited for the eruption.

"Hey, you two. What have you guys been up to?" he asked.

"Oh, nothing, just the regular girl thing, you know. I helped her bring one of her heavy-ass suitcases inside. You didn't tell me that you guys were moving in together." Heaven put her hands on her hips and looked at Cass as if to say he had some explaining to do.

Cass replied, "It just kind of happened that way." His grip on the glass was so tight it shattered in his hand.

Serenity tensed because she was guilty. The tone of his voice made it seem as if he already knew what she had been up to. *Does he know?* she thought in paranoia. She knew her best bet would be to not get involved, to avoid bringing her own skeletons out of the closet.

"Damn, who the fuck done did you wrong?" Heaven asked, jumping back.

"Shut the fuck up, Heaven, before I throw a glass at you! Just leave me the fuck alone for a minute!" Cass waved Serenity's approaching hand away and stormed off to his home office.

"Damn, what the fuck we did? Well, that's my cue to get the fuck up outta here. Bye, nigga, and when you get your head straight, let me know. Bye, Serenity, hope you can put up with that nigga's shit!" Heaven yelled as she walked out, slamming the door behind her.

Serenity's heart began to beat faster. She looked left, then right. Her insides were screaming at her to leave. *That was too close for comfort, and now he's flying off the handle over who knows what,* she thought. *Well, if we gonna play house, then I better act my part!*

She walked into Cass's office and stood close to the door in case he wanted to show his rage. "Umm . . . Cass, . . ." Serenity said in her sweetest voice. "I think I'm gonna go. Here is your key—"

"I'm sorry, someone's stealin' money from the restaurant. I'm pissed at Heaven 'cause that shit happened on her watch," Cass lied, not wanting to create too much friction before he blew everything.

Serenity felt Cass squeeze her hand, and she gave him a tiny smile before squeezing back. She knew that she was playing with fire. She could only hope that she didn't get burned. Serenity wasn't even really settled in Detroit and that evil bitch named "Drama" was already poking her head into her life. *Am I falling for Cass?* she asked herself. She didn't want to believe that she could fall for a man with such ease, but Cass was different. He penetrated her heart almost from the first time she'd met him. He was intriguing and, although she knew that they were moving at the pace of a speeding bullet, she recognized the emotions that were building inside of her. It was official. She belonged to Cass.

That night she decided that she would not mess with Heaven anymore. She liked Cass, and the tiny ache in her heart let her know that there was potential for her to love him. If she wanted any type of future with him, then she would have to keep Heaven at a distance and cut their friendship short.

It was just a phase anyway, just like before, she thought. *I'm not about to do anything to fuck this up. But what am I going to do when I'm horny as hell and he can't give me what I want?* She knew that choosing to be loyal to Cass would be hard. She would be sacrificing sexual pleasure for emotional and financial stability, but it was a trade that she felt was worth it.

Yes, Heaven's out of the picture. I can't do both. I'm not even gay! It was fun while it lasted, but now it's over.

Chapter 20

"Yo, man, what's good?" Stuckey spoke into his phone.

"Tryin' to get this money right. I was just 'bout to call your ass," Shawn P replied.

"Shit, I thought you was coming to see me, my nigga. I ain't here 'cause I want to be. When my next payment comin'?" Stuckey asked.

"I got you. I'ma see you as soon as I land. I should be to you in 'bout two hours, and I think you gonna like what you see and hear from me." Shawn P put Stuckey at ease.

"A'ight, man, I'll see ya," Stuckey said.

"One," Shawn P replied and powered down his phone.

Stuckey looked over at his bed and saw Tootsie sleeping peacefully. When Tootsie got too comfortable and let her mouth get loose, she made him think that Shawn P may just have other agendas besides Serenity.

She reminded him of his mother, looking at her soft, brown, caramel skin. Her naked body lay there with the sheet partially covering her. In his younger days, he would sneak into his mother's room early in the morning and watch her sleep. She would be so tranquil, not screaming, not high, not angered by his presence, not anything; just peaceful. With the time he spent with Tootsie, his feelings for her had grown. He wasn't ready to let her go just yet.

"Yo, wake up. Shawn gonna be here in a while," Stuckey said shaking her.

Tootsie turned over, exposing her succulent breast. Stuckey placed his warm mouth on her nipple, making it react.

"I thought you said Shawn was comin'?" Tootsie reminded him, caressing his head.

"I know, but he ain't gonna be here for a minute, and my dick is hard," Stuckey chanted between sucks.

"Well, I know exactly how to take care of that. Let me taste him, Stuckey. I need it in my mouth." She reached for his crotch and pulled his dick out of his boxers.

"Oh yeah, baby, just like that." Stuckey moaned, allowing Tootsie's mouth to relieve his hard shaft.

Tootsie wrapped her hand around his stiff cock, moving it rapidly up and down as she devoured him in her wet mouth. Stuckey lay back on the bed and let Tootsie please him orally. For the next twenty minutes, she brought him close to his climax three times. When he finally couldn't hold back anymore, he exploded in her mouth. She lapped up every drop, wanting more. Then she stood up and climbed on top of him. His dick was still solid. She used her two fingers to spread her pussy lips open. Then expertly, she slid down on his hard pipe rocking back and forth, increasing her speed as she went.

"Damn, baby, what you tryin' to do to me?" Stuckey asked, grabbing her bouncing round ass in his hands.

"Making my—"

"You making my dick harder. Turn around. Let me see that phat ass of yours jiggle," Stuckey motioned for her to spin around while his snake was still clenched by her wet walls.

Tootsie bounced hard and fast on Stuckey, showing how fast her ass could wiggle. He smacked her hard on her ass, leaving a red imprint of his hand on her right cheek. He sat up with her still bouncing on his dick. In one swift motion, he stood up and she moved like a pro into the position he wanted: doggy-style. She bent over reaching for her toes as he stroked her deep and slow. She tried to push her ass back faster on him, but he protested and grabbed her ass cheeks to slow her down. Increasing his rhythm, he started to pump harder, making sure she screamed every time he rammed her snatch.

"Oh yes, baby, fuck me harder! Take your pussy!" Tootsie screamed as her body inched closer to the wall with his strokes.

"Yeah, you like this dick, don't you? This *my* pussy!" Stuckey yelled out as his climax reached its peak.

With a few more hard, fast strokes, Stuckey let loose all over her round ass. Exhausted, he fell back on the bed breathing heavy. Tootsie did her usual and sucked the last drop of cum out of his penis.

"Tootsie, I want you to be with me. I want you to come away with me after this shit with Shawn P. You with that?" Stuckey asked.

Tootsie looked at his face and could see he was serious. This was not what she wanted. She was just supposed to keep him satisfied. *This is gonna be a problem*, she thought. She didn't respond to his question, hoping he would just forget about it.

Stuckey sat up staring into Tootsie's eyes. "Yo, I asked you a question. Don't you want to be with me?"

"Of course, baby. Wherever you go I'ma be there. Does that answer yo' question?" She started walking to the door of the adjacent room. "I'ma go take a shower and get dressed. I'll be in my room when Shawn P comes." She walked over to him and kissed his lips.

Stuckey glanced at the digital clock beside the bed. *A'ight, I got an hour or two.*

"My dude, what's good?" Shawn P stood at the door with his hand out greeting Stuckey.

Stuckey acknowledged Shawn P and let him enter the room. They took a seat on the sofa. Shawn P placed a small duffel bag on the coffee table.

"That's yours, another fifty grand." Shawn unzipped the bag and motioned for Stuckey to look in it.

"A'ight, that's what I'm talkin' 'bout!" Stuckey said with his eyes wide looking into the bag full of one-hundred-dollar-bill stacks.

"What, you thought I wasn't gonna come through?"

"Nah, but you damn sure took yo' sweet-ass time in bringin' me my shit," Stuckey said.

"I hear you, but you know the deal. I can't be up here like that," Shawn P replied.

"Yeah, a'ight! So, what's the deal? Is this shit gonna be finished soon or what?" Stuckey asked.

"It sure will be. I'ma go get checked in at my hotel, and you can meet me there in 'bout a couple hours; then we can go through how this shit goin' down." Shawn P stood up to leave. Before walking out of the door he said, "Oh yeah, I hope you ain't get attached to homegirl 'cause that bitch gotta go. I got no use for her ass!"

Stuckey closed the door. *He wants her dead too! What the fuck! That shit was not the deal!*

"Yo, you in town?" Cass spoke into his phone.

"No, why?" Iris yawned as she answered.

"'Cause this shit 'bout to go down. You still down to handle that?" Cass asked.

"I'll be on the next flight. I'ma need to make a few calls and handle some things when I get there, but we should be good to go after ten tonight. Talk to you in a couple of hours." Iris hung up the phone.

Cass walked into his bedroom to find Serenity asleep in his bed. He walked out and went into his spare bedroom to lie down. It was about ten in the morning, and he should have been in the restaurant by now, but after what he saw last night he couldn't face Heaven.

How didn't I know? Shit, I did know, just didn't want to admit it! Why didn't she tell me? I need to know if I'm the only one she kept in the dark. Cass's thoughts flew around his mind. He swallowed hard and stood up from the bed. "I gotta go and face her. If I don't, I will never be able to forgive her," he mumbled to himself.

"Heaven, I'm still waitin' for my money. When I'm gonna see it?" Rico asked, stopping Heaven from entering her office.

"Rico, like I told you before, it ain't gonna be six. We can continue to argue 'bout it, and you won't get—"

"Oh no, ain't no arguing 'bout shit. Either you give me what I want or your shit is out in the open with Cass!" Rico walked off, bumping Heaven's shoulder a tiny bit.

Heaven walked into her office and slammed the door. "Who the fuck does that muthafucka think he is?" she asked out loud with anger and frustration.

She walked behind her desk and took a seat. *I know one person that can put a smile on my face!* Heaven pulled out her phone and dialed Serenity.

"I want to see you." Heaven stated as soon as she picked up.

"Ummm . . . Heaven, this can't happen anymore. My feelings for Cass are strong. We can't do this anymore. It was fun, but I'm with Cass. I like him, and I don't want to hurt him. So this thing, whatever me and you are doin', can't happen anymore."

"Cass doesn't care about you, Serenity. I didn't want to tell you, but he been fuckin' just about everything that walks outta that strip club he owns. Why you even actin' that way? Don't you want us both?" Heaven smacked her lips.

Serenity frowned at the words she heard. *I know she's lying. She's just trying to get under my skin,* she thought. "I can't do this with you. It's not worth it. Please, don't call me again," Serenity's words were bitter. She hung up her phone and set it back on the nightstand.

Her phone immediately rang. It was Heaven. She touched IGNORE on the screen. The phone buzzed, alerting her to a picture mail in her inbox. She opened it and a photo of Heaven's pussy displayed across her screen. Serenity's womanhood jumped unexpectedly. She deleted the picture and shook her head. *She just doesn't get the picture,* she thought. Another buzz came in, and she opened that picture. Heaven was sitting at her desk pleasuring herself with a dildo this time.

Stop sending me these fuckin' pictures, bitch! Serenity replied to Heaven.

Serenity shut off her phone and walked into the bathroom. She locked the door behind her and sat on the toilet. Her pussy was so wet from the photos Heaven had sent her. She turned on her phone and opened one of the pictures back up, all the while convincing herself that there was nothing wrong with just looking. A beautiful, pink, juicy cunt filled the screen, and Serenity opened her legs and masturbated to the lovely sight. She rubbed her pearl gently, licking her fingers so that she could taste herself, then putting the wetness on her clit. One finger, two fingers, then three as she pushed them in and out of herself. She tried to think of Cass and she fucked herself, but only Heaven's face came to mind. She rotated her hips and licked her lips. *God, I need my dildo,* she thought. Her fingers just didn't reach deep enough, but she brought herself to an orgasm anyway and creamed all over her hands.

After a shower, Serenity called out for Cass. No one answered. "I guess he went to the restaurant," she said out loud.

Heaven sat at her desk trying to get herself off but couldn't. She pulled down her dress and decided on going to see Serenity. She wasn't going to let her just stop when everything was going so good.

Heaven walked to the parking lot in a gold Balenciaga dress and gold Givenchy pumps. Her hair was pulled high on her head in loose curls and her makeup was on point, covering her imperfections and accenting her assets. She got into her car and decided to stop first at the florist to pick up a dozen yellow roses for Serenity. Heaven passed a jewelry store and couldn't resist picking up a beautiful diamond tennis bracelet to win Serenity back. *Shit, what chick don't like diamonds? This should make her have some second thoughts on us.* Heaven's thoughts shifted in her head. She stepped into the car with roses and jewelry for the one person that could keep her secret until she was ready. *Love her,* she thought with a smile. *Can I actually love her this soon?*

***

Serenity heard the doorbell ring. She rushed to the door and peeked through the window to see a delivery-man standing holding a bouquet of white lilies. She opened the door.

"Hello, Miss, I have a delivery for Serenity White. Can you sign for it here?" the man said.

"I sure can." Serenity signed her name on the paper and took the bouquet out of his hands.

"Thank you, Ms. White. You have a great day," the man said leaving.

Wow, I wonder who these are from. Serenity took the bouquet into the house and set it on the kitchen table. She searched for the card. "Oh my goodness," she whispered in amazement. "This is so sweet."

I'm sorry about last night. I want to make it up to you tonight.

Love, Cass

It was obvious that he felt strongly for her, and she couldn't believe that he was being so good to her. She sat down and picked up her phone to call him.

"You like the flowers?" he asked as soon as he answered the phone.

"I love them, baby," she admitted. "You didn't have to do—"

Before she could get the sentence out of her mouth, Heaven opened the door. She strutted over with flow-ers and a small jewelry box in hand. Serenity hadn't locked the door after receiving the delivery.

"Serenity . . . Serenity, are you there?" Cass asked.

"Oh, um, yeah, I'm here, Cass. I'm sorry, I got dis-tracted," she said motioning to Heaven to keep her mouth shut. She turned around in the chair, and Heav-en placed the yellow roses and jewelry box on the table in front of her.

"Get off the phone," Heaven mouthed sexily. She opened the jewelry box and pulled out the bracelet, then fastened it on Serenity's wrist. Then, Heaven sat on the table and spread her legs wide open. She wore no panties and was freshly waxed.

"I love the flowers, babe," Serenity said. "You're so special. You're too good to me." A tear slipped down her cheek as she reached out to touch Heaven. *How can I be so scandalous?* she asked herself as she opened Heaven's southern lips wide. She had never seen a clit so big.

Heaven could probably put it on any nigga in the city and have them loving it. Serenity was sure that Heaven had the best pussy in the world. Heaven moved her hips back and forth, making Serenity's fingers slip in and out. Then Heaven reached out and pinched Serenity's nipple.

"Cass—I—I've got to go take a shower," she whispered a lie. She closed her eyes as she stroked Heaven some more, then opened her own legs and fingered herself, alternating back and forth. "I have to get ready so I can go get the rest of my stuff," she lied.

"A'ight, ma. I just want you to know that I'm sorry. I know my temper got the best of me, and I just want you to know you don't have to be scared of me, Serenity," he said.

"Talk dirty to me, Cass," Serenity whispered.

"What?" he asked, the intrigue obvious in his voice. He sat at his desk in his office at the restaurant.

"I'm so wet," she moaned. Heaven smiled. Serenity loved being bad, and the fact that she was fucking Heaven while Cass was on the phone with her was erotic.

"You want me to stroke it, baby?" he asked.

Serenity looked in Heaven's eyes and answered, "Yeah, stroke it, Cass. This pussy is yours."

Heaven put both legs on the table and pulled Serenity closer. Her face was close to Heaven's cunt.

"You playing with it?" Cass asked.

"Yeah, I'm playing with it," she said, her fingers slipping in and out of Heaven's pussy. "It's so pretty and wet. You want to hear it?"

"Yeah, ma, let me hear it," he said, his excitement building.

Serenity put the phone close to Heaven's pussy as she continued to finger her. "Shit, it's so juicy and fat," she whispered. She got on her knees. She couldn't take it anymore. She licked that beautiful clit. The tiny bulb in her mouth tasted sweet and smelled fresh. She tongue kissed it as if she were kissing Cass's lips. The phone was still in her hands.

"Damn, Serenity, your pussy sound like it's wet, ma," Cass said, hearing the licking that Serenity was doing to Heaven. Heaven wanted to moan so badly but knew that Cass would hear her. She bit down on her tongue to keep herself from making any noise.

"It's wet, daddy . . . Are you stroking your dick, baby?" Serenity asked.

"Hell, yeah," he whispered. "I'm rubbing it, ma. I want to fuck you. It's brick hard over here. My man is screaming for you."

"So fuck me," she said. "Pretend I'm there. Use your hand."

She sucked and tugged on Heaven's clit. Neither of them had ever experienced an episode so nasty before, but they were loving every minute of it.

"Baby girl, I'm about to nut," Cass said.

"Cum," Serenity said as she torpedoed Heaven's pussy with a stiff tongue. "Cum in my mouth," she commanded. That comment took both Cass and Heaven over the top.

Heaven pulled Serenity's head close and ground into her tongue as if she were riding a dick. She could hear her brother moaning over the phone, turning her on even more.

Serenity was still horny and ready for round two. She didn't even give guilt a chance to creep in. "Was it good?" she asked into the phone, but the way that she was looking at Heaven let Heaven know that the question was really for her.

"You're the best, ma, but I want the real thing when I see you," he said.

"Are you coming home now?" she asked, quickly touching Heaven's nipples.

"Nah, I gotta talk to Heaven so I'ma wait 'til she comes in. A'ight, I'ma hit ya in a few."

"Okay, let me clean up. Thanks for the flowers," she said, then quickly hung up.

She was all in now. She missed eating Heaven's pussy and like a crackhead to a rock, she was chasing that first-time high again. She pulled Heaven off the table and went to the sofa. They got into the 69 position, where they fucked each other like rabbits. She swallowed so much of Heaven's cum, and she came so many times that her pussy was sore, but the two never stopped.

"Serenity," Heaven said between licks.

"Hmm?" Serenity moaned, not wanting anything else but Heaven's tongue satisfying her.

"I want to do this with you. I'm feeling you. I'm feeling this," Heaven admitted.

"Hmm," Serenity moaned. At the moment she was feeling it too. She squeezed Heaven's ass cheeks and put a finger at the tip of her anus. Heaven squirted long and hard all over Serenity's face. The two still did not stop. They were literally addicted to each other and were binging on pussy and ass. They licked each other from hole to hole, then sat up and sucked on each other's breasts. They were naked at this point, and their bodies were aching in a good way.

Facing each other Heaven looked into Serenity's eyes. "How good is this, baby?"

"It's perfect," she admitted. Serenity lay down, and Heaven crawled on top. Their clits were so exhausted, but the slightest touch sent them into orgasms because they were so supersensitive. They humped, bumped, and grinded, their love buttons wrestling between their bodies until they both let out a loud roar. They wanted to continue but couldn't. They were both spent and satisfied.

"I've got to take a shower," Serenity said. "You want to join me?" She was on an orgasmic high, and no matter how much she told herself to stop, her body kept urging her forward.

The two lovers showered together. They fingered each other while washing each other's bodies. They couldn't get enough of each other, kissing and rubbing their soapy bodies together. Their chemistry was undeniable, but it was wrong, and later, Serenity knew she'd feel like shit. *Right now, I'm going to enjoy it though,* she thought.

"What are you doing to me?" Serenity asked.

"Nothing that you don't want me to," Heaven said. She stretched Serenity's pussy as she added more fingers.

Serenity spread her legs to allow better access.

"You like it, don't you?" Heaven continued.

"I love it," Serenity admitted. "But we've got to stop."

"I can't stop now," Heaven admitted. "You're the only one I can be so open with."

Serenity gasped in slight pain and shock as Heaven inserted her thumb into her pussy and balled her hand into a fist.

"Aghh," Serenity purred. "Wait, it's too much," she protested.

"Just relax your pussy. Relax your muscles," Heaven instructed.

Serenity took a deep breath, and then eased her muscles as Heaven worked the fist in and out, slowly. It felt like she was punching her pussy, beating it up. Heaven sucked her engorged clit simultaneously.

Cass was temporarily erased from all of Serenity's thoughts. At that moment, she didn't give a damn if he dropped off the fucking planet. A world full of women who could make her feel like this was what she craved. "Ohh! Shit! God!" she screamed at the top of her lungs. She was so glad that Cass wasn't coming home now.

Heaven smiled as she stood. They both washed once more, then stepped out of the shower. They kissed and flirted while they toweled off in the bathroom. "I don't want to stop this," Serenity finally admitted out loud.

"We don't have to," Heaven said. They were both dressed now, and they kissed the way that lovers do. Serenity was completely turned out.

"I don't want to leave Cass either, though," Serenity said. She knew that she sounded selfish. She wanted the best of both worlds, and after the connection she had just made with Heaven, she didn't want to give her up either. She would choose if she had too, but why did she have to? If she could juggle both, she was going to.

"You don't have to. Nobody has to know. Shit, I don't want nobody to know. What do you think my brother is going to do if he finds out that I like pussy just like him?" Heaven paused. "But, I can see how he loves you, though. Just to let you know, it's more than sex for me."

"I think it's more than sex for me," Serenity replied. "But I'm not ready for all that. I'm not trying to have a relationship with you. I have a relationship with Cass. I'm selfish. I want to have my cake and eat it too."

Heaven nodded and said, "You can eat it anytime. I'm a woman, Serenity. I know what you like because I have the same feelings and emotions you do. No man in the world can make you feel better. Not even Cass."

Serenity understood exactly what Heaven was saying. There was a certain connection, a different type of connection that she had only experienced with Heaven. It was like Heaven was in tune with her needs, wants, and desires. Heaven knew her deepest fantasy without even asking her. She knew how to suck on her nipples without sucking too hard; she knew how to caress her where a man just probed and prodded.

Being with a woman was gentler, more comfortable, but Serenity couldn't see herself living that open lifestyle. She couldn't throw caution to the wind and just be open with her business. Lesbian women were always judged, and Serenity definitely didn't want that. Plus, what would happen when she was afraid? How was a woman supposed to make her feel safe? Which woman was the provider? Which one played the back and took care of home? Sex with a woman was better, but life with a man, a good man, was bliss. A good man was a blessing. A man like Cass was a blessing.

Serenity was in a trance thinking about the pros and cons.

Chapter 21

Cass sat at his desk wondering when Heaven was going to walk in. Finally, he stood and decided to find Rico to inquire.

"Yo, Rico, let me holla at you for a minute."

"A'ight, can I finish restocking the bar?" Rico asked.

"Yeah, you can stock while I talk. Ummm, where is Heaven?" Cass asked.

"She was here since eight this morning. She must of left, but I'm sure she'll be back. Did you try calling her?"

"A'ight. Nah, I ain't call her. I wanna see her when I talk to her," Cass stated in a low tone.

"You want something to drink, Boss?" Rico asked, sensing some frustration.

"Nah, I'm good. Rico, I need to ask you a question about my sister. But I need you to be honest with me," Cass said, then continued, "Is my sister gay?"

Rico choked on his spit reacting to the question. He knew if he answered truthfully, he could kiss his black-mail money good-bye. "Cass, are you serious?" he tried to pretend that he knew nothing.

"Rico, don't play stupid with me. I know you can tell me. She spends most of her time here with yo' ass. You see who she talk to 'round here!" Cass stared at him.

At that moment, Heaven walked in smiling with a huge white lily in her hair. They both watched her as she waved her hand hello and walked to her office without a word. She was on cloud nine. She finally found her perfect intimacy without having her secret out.

"I guess you don't have to answer my question, Rico. You off the hook." Cass left the bar and trailed behind Heaven.

He stood in the doorway of her office. "What up, sis?" Heaven placed her purse on the floor beside her desk and took her seat. "Everything is good. Why?"

"I could see that with that big-ass grin you got on your face," Cass replied.

"Ha-ha, what? You mad that I am? Cass, please don't ruin my mood," Heaven said.

"Nice flower. Where you got it?" Cass's voice got loud.

"Damn, you mad 'cuz I got a flower in my hair? Cass you on some real shit. Get the fuck outta my office." Heaven motioned to the door with her hand and started to retrieve her phone out of her purse.

Cass walked to the door and slammed it shut. He didn't want to play any games. He wanted the truth about everything.

"What the fuck—" she looked up to see Cass standing in front of her desk with an upset look on his face.

"You know the fuckin' problem, you fuckin' bitch! What, you couldn't get no other bitch's pussy to eat?" Cass barked out.

Heaven's face went fire red. "Umm—what—" she stuttered.

"Don't fuckin' stutter now. Tell me why you did it. With all the pussy in this fuckin' state you couldn't find nobody to fuck? I know you was just at my fuckin' house too 'cuz you got that fuckin' flower in your hair! I just sent Serenity those flowers this morning!" Cass snatched the flower out of Heaven's hair and threw it to the floor. "You must've gotten your fuckin' rocks off again!"

"Ah—um, what you mean again—Listen, I haven't done shit with Serenity. And, yes, I was at your house earlier," Heaven lied.

"Heaven, I fuckin' saw you and her! Y'all was fuckin' naked, eatin' pussy in *my* fuckin' bed!" Cass shouted and kicked the chair in front of her desk.

"You saw us naked?"

"You remember when I broke the glass . . . Well, I was there before you met me in the kitchen. How could you do that? How come you ain't tell me you like girls? What the fuck, Heaven, you can't tell me nothin' no more? I'm your fuckin' brother. You my only fuckin' family!" Cass's voice started to crack. The hurt of his sister's secret was devastating news. He could get over the fact that she fucked his woman but couldn't understand why she didn't tell him how she was really livin'.

"Shit, now that I know your ass is fuckin' goin' down that route I'ma make sure I never bring any female around you," Cass said frustrated.

"Cass—I—I don't know what to say," Heaven said, bowing her head.

Heaven was exploring new levels of sexuality, making her body feel things it never had felt before. She was only experimenting with Serenity. She wasn't openly gay, or so she told herself. It wasn't a title that she wore on her sleeve. She wouldn't even call herself bisexual. She was just curious. She was just sowing some wild oats.

"You don't know what to say? Well, I'ma tell you that Serenity ain't gonna be 'round much longer. I'ma headin' to my crib to kick her ass out." Cass kicked the chair again.

Heaven stood up and reached out to him.

"Fuck you," he said. He began to walk away, but Heaven grabbed his arms.

"Bitch, keep your hands off of me. You nasty ho!" he was so livid that he pushed Heaven hard against the desk and stormed out.

Heaven's head hit the corner of the desk with force, and she was dazed. The office turned into one big blur, and a pain seared through her skull. She touched the tender spot on the back of her head and brought back a bloody hand. She attempted to stand but fell back to the ground with her eyelids quickly closing.

***

"Yo, meet me at the hotel in about twenty minutes. I'm leaving the airport now," Iris spoke into her phone.

"Yeah, a'ight," Cass spoke into his phone, turning the key in the ignition. He touched END on his phone, then dialed Serenity.

"Hey, baby . . ."

"Are you dressed?" Cass asked.

"Yeah, why?"

"Why don't you meet me in half an hour at that little cozy restaurant we discovered a few weeks back," Cass insisted.

"Actually, I wanted to go scoop Heaven up so we could go have dinner together. We wanted to go check out that new movie by Tyler Perry too. You're welcome to join," Serenity said.

"Dinner with Heaven, huh?" Cass fought the urge to bust her in her lie. He knew exactly what kind of dinner she was planning. "Heaven actually has to work the celeb dinner party tonight, so she ain't gonna be able to hang with you. So meet me there in thirty," Cass said in an authoritative tone.

"All right, since you put it like that, I guess I have to," Serenity said unsure of why he was acting the way he was.

"Yeah, well, I'll see you there then." Cass hung up the phone.

"Okay, bye."

Cass pulled up to the valet at the Ritz hotel. He stepped out of his car and walked into the hotel toward the bar. He could see Iris sitting at the bar upon entering the room. He took a seat next to her.

"Want something to drink?" Iris asked.

"Nah, I'm good. Let's just get to the business," Cass insisted.

"Yeah, well, you gotta tell me where you gonna be. And, once you let homeboy in, you can call me; then I can take it from there."

"So, I guess that's it, then. When should I expect my money from you?" Cass asked.

"Give me 'bout a week or two. I got it all set up," Iris replied.

"A'ight. You know where she going?" Cass asked, almost showing concern.

"Why you asking me that? You better not be punkin' out on me. That shit won't be a good look for you or me, understand me?"

"You right. I don't care. I'll text you in a few hours. It's time to put on a show." Cass stood up and left.

Cass's phone buzzed as he entered his car. "Yo, what's the deal?"

"I should be asking you that question. You know time is of the essence," Shawn P said.

"Well, I'ma call you and let you know where," Cass recited.

"Call me and let me know where? What the fuck you think this is? This shit ain't no fuckin'—You know what? Forget all that shit. I'ma text you an address of a hotel. You take her there. Make sure you talk to my man Abdul, a'ight?" Shawn P said reducing his temper.

"Cool. One." Cass hung up the phone.

Shawn P pressed END on his phone and quickly dialed another number. "Yo, Abdul, I need a favor. My man gonna come by to get a room for the night. Just make sure he gets room five. You ain't change the locks, right?"

"Nah, you still got that key . . . Damn, I guess you got a little party goin' on tonight. Damn, son, I just don't know how you get over on 'em girls like that." Abdul laughed.

"Stupid bitches, that's all. You see, the trick is get 'em comfortable with my man, then I just swing by when the time is right . . . then, boom, full-fledged freak party!" Shawn P lied.

"One day, you gonna have to let me in on the party. You know what I mean? 'Cause the wife is lame as a log," Abdul exclaimed.

"Bet, I can make that happen. A'ight, my nigga, be safe. One." Shawn P hung up the phone.

"Hello," Carla answered.

"Can we meet up sometime this week, just to talk. I don't want us to be like this," Serenity said while driving to meet Cass.

"Be like what, Serenity? You left. I didn't tell yo' ass to leave." Carla smacked her lips irritated.

"Why you actin' like that? All I want to do is mend our relationship. You the only family I got. If you don't wanna talk, then fine. I guess I'ma have to keep callin' you until you ready." Serenity hung up the phone, annoyed by her sister's response.

"Why the fuck she callin' my ass? Why she ain't call her fuckin' man?" Carla asked out loud. She threw her phone across the room. It smashed against the wall. "Well, I guess I ain't gettin' called back any time soon, so fuck it! Fuck this shit. I'm fucking goin' back to Chicago. At least I can make some money there."

Serenity desperately wanted her sister in her life, but it seemed that Carla didn't want to be there. It still boggled her mind about why her sister wouldn't be happy for her. *Cass is a good guy. I just gotta get her to see that,* Serenity thought, pulling into the lot of the restaurant.

Chapter 22

Stuckey looked over at Tootsie admiring her phat ass in some Seven jeans. He knew what he had to do. He thought about how he felt when his mother died. He was alone and had been for a long time. Stuckey wanted a new life, and he wanted it with Tootsie.

"Tootsie, would you do anything for me?"

"Yes, Stuckey," she said without hesitating.

"A'ight." Stuckey went into the safe in his room and walked back to Tootsie with a 9 mm. "Take this."

"Why are you giving me a gun? Is it that time already?" Tootsie asked, surprised.

"You know how to use it, right?" Stuckey questioned, not even bothering to answer her.

"Stuckey, yes, I know how to use a gun. Don't you know I've killed before?" Tootsie said without thinking.

He looked at her a little surprised. He didn't know that she had killed before. The only knowledge Shawn P provided him with was she was on parole. Actually, he knew nothing about her past. She never talked about it with him, only what she wanted the future to be like with him.

"Oh, so that's why you on parole, huh?"

"It ain't even like—"

Stuckey cut her off, "Well, it's all good, shorty. I like you for who you are now, not who you was back then. That's water under the bridge."

"So, why give me the gun? Ain't you scared I might shoot you and say fuck all this revenge and power-trippin' shi—"

"Revenge? Power? What the fuck are you talkin' 'bout?" Stuckey grabbed her by the shoulder and force-fully sat her down. "Tootsie, I'ma ask you this just once, and it better be the answer I'm lookin' for!"

"Stuckey, why are you actin' this way? Aren't we here to do a job? I wanna get paid and get the fuck up outta here," Tootsie said, trying to hold on to her composure. Her finger was now on the trigger as the gun sat on the table.

"Tootsie, my heart is not a game. Do you want to be with me? Are you willin' to have my back no matter what?" Stuckey stared at her.

"Yes, Stuckey, how many times do we have to go through this?" she asked, trying not to reveal her true intentions. Shawn P made her endure quite enough, and she was leaving Detroit today—no matter what. Even if it meant blowing all of what she had done.

"You're going to kill Shawn P so we can get the fuck up out of Dodge," he demanded.

"Kill Shawn P? How?" Tootsie's eyebrows rose.

"I just gave yo' ass the gun! Don't play games with me! You gonna know what to do!" Stuckey motioned for her to stand up and head out.

He followed behind her toting his Glock 21 tucked into the back of his pants.

Cass sat in his chair sipping on a glass of water wait-ing for Serenity to arrive. He really needed a drink, but his head could do with the clarity. *Should I really do this shit? Do I want to do this shit? So what she fucked Heaven? I can't let that shit come between me and my sister!*

Serenity walked into the restaurant to see Cass appearing grim. His gaze was broken when Serenity came to the table. She kissed his lips and sat down.

"Everything all right, baby?"

"Yeah, yeah, just thinking, but now that you're here I can forget 'bout all that stuff! Are you hungry?" Cass said cheerfully, disguising his shaken demeanor.

"A little. Did you order already?" Serenity asked.

"Nah, let me see if I can get the waitress's attention." Cass locked eyes with a server and waved her over.

They ordered a couple of appetizers and a bottle of champagne. Serenity protested at first but decided, why not? After the hot session she had earlier, she thought having a few drinks would make her feel better.

He was the type of man that bitches would kill to have, and here she was playing games. She felt like shit. It wasn't love, but it was something. Maybe a deep infatuation, but whatever it was, it was strong and pulling her in.

"Serenity, tell me a little about your past. You never mentioned what brought you to Detroit." Cass wanted—hoped for—the truth.

"Baby, I really don't like to go backward. Can't we talk 'bout our future instead?" Serenity asked, feeling a little tipsy.

Cass nestled himself closer to her, feeling the effects of the alcohol. "Baby, if we don't talk 'bout the past, how we gonna have a future? Shit, for all I know, you could be a murderin' bitch!" His tone got loud unexpectedly.

Serenity couldn't believe the quick change in Cass's voice. She didn't know what he knew, but she didn't want him to start digging up her past. She could sense his aggression. She did what she knew best.

"Come on, follow me. I got something for you." she whispered in his ear.

She walked to the bathroom. It was a small restaurant, and it wasn't crowded. Serenity slipped into the bathroom with Cass on her heels. She dropped to her knees and awakened his manhood with her luscious lips. She loved sucking dick and loved the size of him in her mouth. Cass could last all day with oral, but as soon as he got inside of her wetness, he instantly exploded.

He pulled her to her feet and pressed her face against the bathroom wall. Quickly, he lifted her skirt and ripped her thongs off. Without a moment of hesitation, he inserted himself from behind and pumped in and out, slowly.

"Agh," he grunted with each thrust.

The shit was feeling too good, but Serenity didn't want to get her hopes up. She had already come to terms that sex would never be the highlight of their relationship. She was getting into it because he was hitting her spot, but as soon as she began to throw the pussy back at him, he came, long and hard, inside of her. Now, he kissed the back of her neck.

"Come on, let's leave. I want you to sit on my face. I want my dick in your sweet pussy longer than this," he said in a low voice.

She knew she had some good pussy. Unfortunately, for Cass, the only compliment she could truly give was that his size was more than a mouthful. They would be the perfect couple if only he could satisfy her sexually, but she knew that no relationship was perfect and the complaint that she had with Cass wasn't big enough for her to walk away.

Chapter 23

Stuckey pulled up and parked across the street from the hotel Shawn P told him to be at. He looked at Tootsie and could see a worrisome stare on her face.

"Yo, you good?" he asked.

"Yeah, yeah, I'm good. But how do you know that Shawn P will want me to pull the trigger?" Tootsie exhaled.

"Trust me. He ain't gonna want to pull that trigger. He ain't that stupid. Yeah, he might beat her ass, but to kill her himself—No, he ain't gonna do that," Stuckey said, sure of himself.

"A'ight. So what? Just go in there with guns blazin'? I don't know 'bout that . . ." her voice trailed off.

"Tootsie, you told me that you want to be with me. This is what you have to do to prove your loyalty to me," Stuckey said, never taking his eyes off the hotel. He could see the entrance and the parking lot in perfect view.

"Stuckey . . . I have to tell you something," Tootsie said almost in a childlike manner.

"I'm listening," he said, curious to find out what she's been keeping from him.

"Umm . . . Shawn . . . He . . . He—"

"Can you just spit that shit out? I don't like to be beat in my head. If you going to pull the trigger, then pull that shit!"

"Shawn P wants me to kill you." Tootsie closed her eyes, not knowing if she would ever be able to open them back up again.

"Are you fuckin' around? 'Cause this ain't the time for that shit!" He took his eyes off the hotel and in one fluid motion, he reached for his gun, took the safety off, and placed it on his lap.

Tootsie knew the decision to tell him the truth could go either way. She could be shot dead where she sat, or he would rush into that hotel and kill Shawn P out of pure hatred for playing him in the worst way.

Stuckey wanted to pistol-whip her across her face for telling him some stupid shit like that. But he knew it was the truth because her face and body were tense.

Tootsie's lips began to quiver without tears filling her eyes.

"Oh, so that's how he wanna play the game? A'ight. We gonna see who playin' who soon," Stuckey said with anger. He turned to her and said, "Gimme, your gun. You gonna listen, and listen carefully. I'ma tell you how this shit gonna go down!"

Tootsie was relieved that what she had just told him wasn't the death of her.

Serenity was feeling just right. She didn't think she was drunk, but she was. All she needed was a good nut. She only hoped that Cass wouldn't let her down this time. As Cass drove to their next destination she couldn't keep her hands off him. She rubbed on his cock. She guided his fingers to her flesh.

To his surprise, he almost fit his fist in her hole, which made him hornier. "Oh, damn, baby, I didn't know it was like that. We gonna have to pull over and get a room at one of these hotels, 'cause you just teasin' a nigga," Cass said as he played with her wetness.

"Come on, baby, just pull over and let me climb on top of you, please . . ." Serenity didn't know if it was the champagne or him that made her such a freak.

Champagne or not, Serenity had always been a freak. She was in complete denial.

Suddenly, she realized that Cass was pulling into the parking lot of some rundown hotel. Her entire composure changed.

"Cass, we are *not* goin' in there! It don't even look like they clean the sheets in there. Please, you can't be serious," she protested.

"Serenity, I want to fuck, and this here is the only hotel for miles. So, we doin' this here. Shit, ain't nobody said we gotta fuck on the bed," Cass reminded her. He kissed her passionately as his fingers moved in and out of her warm, inviting flesh.

"Ahh, baby, now you teasing me. Go get the room. I need you inside me now," Serenity said, panting.

Cass rushed out of the car and entered the hotel. He approached the front desk. "Hey, is Abdul 'round?" he asked the older woman behind the desk.

"Mmm. Let me get him for you."

A 250-pound, black, bald-headed man walked out to greet him.

"What up? My man Shawn P said to come see you 'bout a room," Cass stated.

"Oh, yeah"—he turned to the older woman—"Mom, why don't you go get somethin' for us to eat from that barbeque place down the block. I feel for some ribs."

The elderly lady stuck her hand out and smiled. Abdul placed a fifty-dollar bill in her hand and shooed her away. Cass stood there in silence waiting for the woman to leave.

"All right, let's see, room five. You staying the night, right?" Abdul asked, smiling.

"Umm . . . yeah, yeah. How much I owe you?" Cass pulled out a wad of cash waiting for his answer.

"That will be one-fifty even. I assume you want the full package," Abdul said, grinning from ear to ear.

"Full package?" Cass wondered out loud. He couldn't think this dump would have any packages, yet alone a full package. "Yeah, full package."

Abdul handed Cass the key card and told him he could enter through the back door so no one would see his lady friend.

Before Cass reached the car he sent a quick text to Iris letting her know what room they would be in. He also called Shawn P to let him know it was on and poppin'.

Rico was busy at the bar and noticed that Heaven didn't make her normal walk-through before the place got packed. He waved over another bartender and told her to cover for him. Then he walked directly to Heaven's office. He could see that the door was slightly ajar. Rico knocked on the door. He heard no response. He waited a few seconds before knocking again. Still no answer. Now he was pissed because he wasn't about to take her post and do his job too. He opened the door wider.

Rico let out a big gasp and ran over to Heaven, who was lying on the floor looking lifeless.

"Heaven, Heaven, are you okay? Heaven, please open your eyes!" Rico screamed as he shook her.

Heaven began to open her eyes. Her head throbbed. "What—what happened?"

"Don't move! Just lie there. Should I call the ambulance? Where are you hurt? You're bleeding, Heaven!" Rico shouted.

Heaven tried to move again, slowly this time. "Can you get me some ice, Rico? My head really hurts."

Rico moved swiftly and returned with a bag full of ice. He gently placed it on her bloody head. "Oh my God, Heaven, were we robbed or somethin'? Who did this?"

Heaven let out a slight laugh. "No, we weren't robbed, Rico. All the money is still in the safe. Damn, my head hurts!"

"Um, you're bleeding. You know that, right?" Rico reminded her, worried. "Who did this, Heaven?" Rico asked again.

"No one. I slipped and bumped my head," Heaven lied.

"Why the fuck are you lying? The last person in here with you was Cass. Did *he* do this?" Rico's voice now sounded annoyed by her bold-faced lie.

"Look, don't worry about it"—she slowly rose to her feet and clutched the chair in front of her—"it's my business!" she lashed out.

"Are you serious? I can't fuckin' believe you. I probably saved your fuckin' life comin' in here. You know what? You right; it is your fuckin' business. You handle that shit. After tonight, consider me an ex-employee. If I didn't have a heart I would leave right now!" Rico stormed out of her office.

Why does he always have to be so fuckin' dramatic? It was just a slight disagreement between family. What fuckin' concern is it of his anyway? Shit, I gotta call Serenity and tell her that the cat is outta the bag.

"Stuckey, they should be there. I just got the call. Did you see her?" Shawn P asked.

"Yeah, they just got here. So, I'ma leave the other car in the alley next to the hotel. The key is in the glove, a'ight?" Stuckey said quickly.

"Yeah, that'll work. Um, so that *other* problem we talked 'bout, I know how I want it handled," Shawn P said.

"Oh yeah, I think I already know what you got in mind. Why should you be the one? I'm already reading the words on the page," Stuckey said, keeping his anger hidden.

"That's why I like you. You already know what I'm thinkin'. I'ma call you when I'm ready. One." Shawn P hung up the phone smiling from ear to ear. *Three birds, one stone! Can't help but to pat myself on the back!* He laughed out loud at his thoughts.

Chapter 24

"Come on, baby, I want you!" Serenity whispered into Cass's ear as they rode the elevator.

Cass threw her against the elevator wall and kissed her roughly. His manhood was already saluting and needed attention—hers.

They reached the third floor and the elevators opened. Cass picked Serenity up, holding her bare ass cheeks in his hands. He already got rid of her panties, so it was an easy entry. He continued to kiss her on her lips and neck until they reached the room door. He noticed a DO NOT DISTURB sign hanging from the doorknob. Quickly, he set her down and reached into his pocket for the key card.

The room was dark as they entered. He didn't bother to switch the light on. Instead, he undressed her. After removing her dress from over her head, he kissed her breasts gently. He sucked on her nipples like a newborn baby.

Serenity started to moan. There was a fire lit between her legs that she just couldn't put out.

His lips pressed against her clitoris. She rotated her ass and humped his mouth standing in the dark.

Serenity's thoughts drifted to Heaven. Her clit grew larger just thinking about her. Her fantasy was to do them both at the same time, but she knew that it would never happen. It was just that—a fantasy. Her life had become one long porno movie, and she had no objections as long as the shit didn't hit the fan.

"Daddy's going to take care of you, and you're going to take care of daddy." Cass stepped out of his jeans and pulled off his shirt, revealing his big black dick. "Suck it, Serenity."

He pushed her down slowly until she was kneeling in front of him and she began to suck his dick, taking him all the way into the back of her throat and twisting his long shaft as she salivated and hummed. Cass's head fell back in satisfaction.

Her words plagued her brain. *I want dick and dick only.*

The words taunted her and echoed over and over again in her head. But she wanted another female's touch—Heaven's.

"Get on all fours," he instructed. After she obeyed, he inserted his dick and sexed her slowly from behind.

Serenity played with her pussy as he pumped his hard rod into her. Ironically, Cass hadn't cum yet, and at the rate he was pounding her, she didn't think he was close. *Wow, he really gettin' it in like he ain't never gonna tap it again!* she thought.

Cass was beating her pussy up, and the shit was feeling good. She wanted to slow it up. Her pussy had been receiving attention most of the day, and with Cass pounding on her like a newly sprung jailbird, she wouldn't last long.

"Cass, baby, please . . . Let's go to the bed . . . My knees are raw," Serenity finally spoke.

He pulled out his dick and smacked her hard on her ass. "Come on, get up!"

Serenity didn't like his tone. She felt as if she were his property and his pleasure was the only thing important.

Cass followed behind her, leaving all their clothes on the floor. He got to the bed and lay on his back. Serenity climbed on top of him.

"Eat it, baby, please," she begged.

Cass didn't protest. He took her entire pussy into his mouth and sucked it as if he were hungrily devouring a summer peach.

"Aghh," Serenity moaned.

He continued to suck on her white pearl. Serenity felt that her entire day was something straight out of a porno flick. If there had been cameras, lights, and a director calling out "action," Serenity, undoubtedly, would have been dubbed an instant star.

"Shit, daddy, yeah, baby, here it comes . . . Ahhh," Serenity exclaimed.

Creeping slowly, he heard soft moans coming from another room. The closer he got, the more turned on he became. The moaning became louder. The door was not closed, and the room was dimly lit. He stood watching Serenity feeding her pussy into her lover's face with her face against the headboard. Her ass jiggled just right. His dick instantly became harder.

He inched closer without a sound and waited for that moment of ecstasy. As soon as he heard that moan of pure pleasure, his hand reached out and instantly snatched Serenity off the bed and threw her onto the floor toward a corner of the room against the wall.

"Ahhhhhh! What the fuck! Call the police! Call nine-one-one, quickly!" Serenity screamed, hoping that there was no one else with the intruder.

"Oh no, bitch, ain't nobody"—his hands gripped her throat—"calling not a motherfuckin' soul," he said with a calm, deadly voice. He reached above her head and turned up the light in the room.

Serenity tried to get up and run, but he only used his huge hands to slap her down like a bothersome fly.

She tried to study his face to figure out where, or if, she knew this person. *I don't see my baby*, she scanned the room.

"Please, just take what you want and leave. I won't call the police. Please just leave us alone." Serenity began sobbing and covered her face.

"Ahh, shut the fuck up, bitch, you was just screaming"—he waved his hands in front of his face like a little girl—"a fucking minute ago to call the police. Stop fuckin' lyin'. Ho, I don't want nothing from your ass. I already got my own, you fuckin' typical dumb trick. I ain't fuckin' here to rob you. Look at me, you cunt. Don't put your head down. Open yo' fuckin' eyes, bitch, or you want me to do it?"

Serenity turned around not lifting her head, removed her hands covering her face, and opened her eyes. Her tears made everything look cloudy, and her head was spinning. She slowly moved her head up enough to see this monster before she died.

"Don't I look"—he stepped back and flashed his famous smile—"a little familiar?"

"But . . . but . . . where is . . ." Serenity stuttered to plea with him.

She closed her eyes and began crying and wishing this was just another nightmare and she would wake up soon. She felt a soft hand gently wiping her tears. She was now inches from his face and spoke with sincerity. "I don't know you. We have never met before. I think you have the wrong person," she cried louder. "Please, let me go . . . please!"

"Bitch, what the fuck you mean you don't know me?" He smacked her hard, causing blood to spew from her lips.

"I don't know who the fuck you are! I have never seen you before. Please just let me go. I will—" Serenity's loud pleas were cut short by another smack across her face.

"Listen, baby girl, you took something from me that I will never be able to replace," he spoke in a low, sultry tone, almost seductive, "and that shit you gonna fuckin' pay for."

"But . . . but . . . where is . . ." Serenity stuttered to plead with him.

"Your man? Let's just say you ain't with him anymore! What you think? I wasn't gonna come after you?" he chuckled. "You might as well come give me a taste of that pussy too! I want to see why my sister died for it!" He lashed out, hovering over her naked body, staring at her neatly shaved pussy.

"Please . . ." Serenity tried a heartfelt plea one more time.

"Suck my dick!" Shawn P demanded.

Serenity's mouth was instantly hit by Shawn's semi-hard dick. "Put this shit in yo' mouth and suck it!"

Serenity didn't want to, but if this was the only way for her to stay alive, then so be it.

Shawn P exploded on her face, then threw a box of tissues at her to wipe his cum off.

She jumped when the box hit her head, then slowly opened her eyes and inched to the tissue box. Serenity pulled the box apart, frustrated and angry. *How could Cass do this to me? Who is this Grim Reaper?*

"You sure you don't know me?" He flashed a cheesy smile as he wiped the tip of his dick.

"No, I don't fuckin' know you!" she yelled at the top of her lungs.

He smacked her hard across her face, causing blood to spew from her lips. She now looked like she was in the ring with Rocky Balboa for thirteen rounds.

"Well, the least I could do is introduce myself . . . Hello, Serenity. I'm Shawn P . . . Sadie's brother," his voice said in a playful tone.

Serenity's heart sank. Her body was defeated. This was the end. All of her wants were now shut down for good.

"Shawn P . . . I . . . I . . ." Serenity's words wouldn't develop. Her fears made her bow her head and sob uncontrollably, rocking her naked, hurt body.

Shawn P sent a text to Stuckey. A few minutes later, Tootsie entered the room with Stuckey.

"You stupid bitch! Why did you kill my only love?" Tootsie couldn't control herself and leaped at Serenity with her fist connecting with Serenity's right cheek.

"But—What are you doin' here?" Serenity asked, confused, looking at the woman she knew as Debbie. She lowered her head. "Don't kill me! Please don't kill me!" Serenity was now aware that her situation had just become worse.

Tootsie pulled out her 9 mm and put it to Serenity's head. "Bitch, now you gonna die!"

Shawn P stood there enjoying all the hurt Serenity was going through. And now his plan would become reality. "Kill that bitch, Tootsie!" He turned around to Stuckey and motioned for him to kill Tootsie afterward.

When Serenity heard the name Tootsie, the taste of vomit rose from the depths of her stomach into her mouth.

Stuckey looked at Shawn P and nodded with a smile. "Now!"

Tootsie heard Stuckey and knew that it was now or never. She swiftly turned the gun on Shawn P and pulled the trigger, sending the bullet through his chest. He dropped to the floor instantly, pressing his hand against his chest and sucking in as much air as he could, hoping it wasn't his last.

Stuckey walked over to Shawn P and whispered, "What? You thought you could play me, muthafucker? Guess what, nigga? I got yo' money, and now I'ma let your bitch go!"

"Yo, Stuck . . . I thought . . ."

"You thought wrong, nigga." Stuckey put his Glock to Shawn P's temple and fired a single shot.

Blood, brains, hair—splattered everywhere.

Tootsie freaked out. The images of her shooting Rock came back to haunt her. Her gun fell from her hands.

"Tootsie, you good?" Stuckey spoke to her.

"Stuckey, promise me you won't leave me . . . promise me . . ." Tootsie's eyes filled with tears.

"Tootsie, grab the gun. We gotta go. Now!" Stuckey shook her from her trancelike state.

Tootsie grabbed the gun. Unfortunately for Serenity, her sobs brought Tootsie back to reality. Her hands shook aiming the gun at Serenity. "I'ma kill your ass, you stupid bitch!"

"Tootsie," Stuckey shouted, "don't do it! We don't have the time for this bitch. She ain't worth shit. Don't you want to be with me? If you want to be with me, let's go, now!"

"But . . . She killed her . . . I got to—"

"Tootsie, stop this shit!" Stuckey stepped closer. He could see Tootsie's emotions weren't in order, and he didn't want to get caught up 'cause of her foolish actions. *I can't fuck with this bitch. She's fuckin' psycho,* he thought.

Tootsie took the butt of the gun and slammed it against Serenity's head, causing her to become dazed.

Stuckey grabbed the gun out of Tootsie's hand, then tucked it into the front of his pants. He grabbed her arm, pushing her toward the door. He took his Glock and stuck it in the back of his pants. "Let's fuckin' go, now!"

Serenity inched back against the wall and said a silent prayer for her life.

As Stuckey opened the door, to his surprise, a woman appeared in front of him. At first glance he thought it was the maid, but he quickly remembered seeing the DO NOT DISTURB sign on the door.

Before he could react, the woman brandished a gun with a silencer. She pumped two shots into his chest, and he fell back like a stick of dead wood.

Iris backed Tootsie into the room. "Damn, well, I done hit the fuckin' lottery. I got a two-for-one special. I better make this quick," she said under her breath.

Iris picked up a dress off the floor and threw it at Serenity. "If you want to live, get dressed now!" Iris looked at her watch. She was running out of time. She looked at Tootsie. "Don't do nothin' stupid 'cause you'll end up like him!" Iris pointed to Stuckey's dead body lying by the door.

Tootsie's lip began to tremble. "He had a lot of money. I know where it is. Just let me go!"

"Yeah, well, help me get this bitch up outta here then," Iris barked.

Tootsie did as she was told and rushed Serenity to her feet and toward the door.

"Your life will change now that I'm in it," Iris added to their fears.

Serenity's eyes were filled with tears, and her face was bloody. She could hear her phone ringing. She instantly knew it was Heaven by the ringtone. Her body got tense, and her movement became still.

"No, you don't. Keep it movin'," Iris said, rushing them both out the door to the nearest staircase.

Serenity slowly walked down the stairs with thoughts crowding her mind. *Did Heaven betray me too? Why did Cass just leave me there to die? Why didn't I listen to my sister? What is Tootsie doing here? She's supposed to be doing twenty to life in a maximum facility back in D.C.! What the hell has my curiosity got me into this time?*

"Come on, bitches, get in the car. Let's ride!" Iris hollered motioning the women to get into the backseat of a black Audi A8 with the sounds of sirens approaching the scene. "Trini, let's get the fuck out of here," Iris said to the driver after shutting the door.

Serenity gazed out the window, terrified by the harsh results of her rash decisions. Her inability to subdue her urges got her in a deadly situation. She didn't know if she had a future. Her only wish was to see her sister one last time.

ORDER FORM
URBAN BOOKS, LLC
78 E. Industry Ct
Deer Park, NY 11729

Name:(please print):_____

Address: _____

City/State: _____

Zip: _____

QTY	TITLES	PRICE

Shipping and handling-add $3.50 for 1st book, then $1.75 for each additional book.
Please send a check payable to:
Urban Books, LLC
Please allow 4-6 weeks for delivery